# REA

## ACPL

**DISCARDED**

P9-BIO-373

4-22-96

## DO NOT REMOVE
## CARDS FROM POCKET

## ALLEN COUNTY PUBLIC LIBRARY
## FORT WAYNE, INDIANA 46802

You may return this book to any agency, branch,
or bookmobile of the Allen County Public Library.

DEMCO

# 96 TEARS

Also by Doug J. Swanson

*Big Town*
*Dreamboat*

# 96 TEARS

# Doug J. Swanson

HarperCollins*Publishers*

FIRST EDITION

*Designed by Nina Gaskin*

Library of Congress Cataloging-in-Publication Data

Swanson, Doug J., 1953–
   96 tears / Doug Swanson. — 1st ed.
     p.  cm.
   ISBN 0-06-017511-7
   1. Private investigators—Texas—Dallas—Fiction. 2. Dallas (Tex.)—
Fiction. I. Title.
PS3569.W2682A615    1996
813' .54—dc20                             96-13265

96 97 98 99 00 ❖/HC 10 9 8 7 6 5 4 3 2 1

# 1

She wore eyelashes that had been glued on, and they lay across her lids like furry black caterpillars. Her brows were thin arcs drawn with pencil. The man studied her pile of teased blonde hair and thought, You could dye that pink and sell it as cotton candy at the state fair.

"Here's the deal," she said, raising an unlit cigarette to crimson lipstick with a jangle of gold bracelets. "I'm wondering if my little girl just might be making this whole damn thing up."

Jack Flippo sat in the front parlor of this big house in North Dallas and tried to guess the woman's age. Somewhere in her early fifties, but hard to tell with all the paint. She had tight black leather pants over hips that looked to have stayed fairly trim. Her black top, heavy with fringe, sequins, and rhinestones, was cut low. She looked like Zsa Zsa Gabor by way of Ardmore, Oklahoma.

"Mrs. Plunkett," Jack said. "Tell me what—"

"Hey, it's Sherri." She winked. "And that's Sherri with an *i*, by the way."

Sherri with an *i* had called Jack the afternoon before, telling him right away she had picked his name out of the Yellow Pages but she was sure he was a damn good private investigator and he could come see her to prove it.

Jack had been sitting across the room from her for ten minutes now, and still had no idea what she wanted from him. He was about to ask when she said, "Hell of a thing to say your own daughter could be lying, your own flesh and blood. I know that, baby, you don't have to say it. But that's what I think. You didn't ask, but I'm letting you know it all up front. That's the way I do business. I step on the gas and come straight at you. My late husband, Omer Plunkett? He used to say, Sherri never puts no Vaseline on it."

Jack was watching her light her cigarette when his eye snagged on her diamond ring. He could pawn that and live for six months. Sherri set her jeweled lighter on the table next to her and shook some more expensive noise out of the bracelets. She looked at Jack and said, "Omer died last year. Had a heart attack on a trip to Las Vegas."

"I'm sorry."

"He was in a hot tub when it happened." She blew a jet of smoke from the corner of her mouth. "Him and two keno girls."

Jack cleared his throat. "I'm sorry about that, too."

"Omer left me three million." Sherri smiled, the lipstick smearing on her teeth.

After a few seconds Jack said, "You were telling me about your daughter."

"She's visiting me from California, I tell you that already?"

Jack shook his head.

"Sandra's a sweet little girl," Sherri said, "but some of these stories is wild, wild stuff. You want to hear one? Last week at the club, she played some tennis while I had a cocktail or two. I'm talking with some lady friends, okay? Sandra finishes her game and goes on back to the dressing room to change. Then—baby, you're not gonna believe this, you listening? A few minutes later, Sandra come in the bar, still in her tennis clothes. She's got something in her hand. Guess what it is?"

Jack waited for the answer.

"Go ahead, guess," Sherri said. "What's in her hand?"

"Her tennis racket."

"Shit, I wish . . . Here's what happened, see if you can figure this out. Sandra says, 'He's after me again.' I ask her, 'What're you talking about, hon?' She says, 'This,' and she sticks her hand my way. She's holding a pair of black silk panties, and they look like they went through the Disposall."

Jack blinked a couple of times. "I missed something here."

Sherri pulled hard on the cigarette and blew the smoke out in a hurry. "Are you listening, baby? I'm saying they was all sliced up. The panties, I'm talking about. Like somebody'd took a razor to them. I asked Sandra, 'What in the world happened?' She starts shaking and says, 'It's that man, he's after me.'"

"What man?"

"Bless your heart. Same question I had. Along with this one: Tell me how some crazy nut slips into the locker room at Preston Bend Country Club in broad daylight and cuts up a girl's lacies. You want to ask some questions? Ask that one."

"Did you report this to the police?"

"So they could do what? Send out the underwear squad?" Sherri cackled, head back and mouth wide open, a show of gold crowns. Her laugh sounded as if it had been hanging in a smokehouse next to a couple of country hams. "Baby, if you knew what I know about the police, you wouldn't ask that. Some time when we're just sitting around, you and me? Ask Sherri about the police, I'll tell you some stories. Don't think I won't."

Jack took a breath and looked around the room. The carpet was red. So was the heavy, overstuffed furniture. The walls were papered in a textured red. Six or seven large paintings of race-horses hung in a row. The only other portrait in the room was a life-size job of a much younger Sherri wearing nothing but a strategically draped feather boa.

"I'll pay you a thousand dollars a day," Sherri said.

Jack pulled his gaze from the painting and looked at the real thing. She was smiling at him again. "I don't charge that much," he said.

"Find out if somebody really is after my Sandra, that's what Sherri wants. That's all you have to do. Just you, no police. Find out if it's true or not. A thousand a day, take it or leave it. Come on, baby, say yes so I can fix us some vodka cocktails to celebrate."

It was just past eight in the morning. Jack turned down the drink but took the job.

# 2

As Jack left the big house in North Dallas that morning, Sherri gave him a photograph. "Here's my little girl," she said. The picture was of a woman in her early thirties.

It wasn't one of those out-of-focus family snaps with a birthday cake in the foreground, the kind detectives and cops sometimes got. Instead: an eight-by-ten glossy in black and white. A professional glamour shot with bare shoulders, light glinting off dark hair, and a suggestive pout. "My little Sandra," Sherri said.

Sherri's little Sandra looked like the girl next door, if you lived in a neighborhood where everyone slept around. Below the photo, in bold black letters, was "Sandra Danielle, Co-Star of SpanWorld Productions Syndicated Mega-Hit DOUBLE OR NOTHING."

Jack, who found himself with some empty evenings lately, had caught the show a couple of times on Channel 27. It featured the exploits of Stryker Double, an ex-cop from Philadelphia who had moved to Florida to set up Double's Fishing Supplies & Guide Service.

Every week Stryker Double had to stop catching pompano long enough to solve a murder. Florida was probably full of fishing crimebusters, you found them everywhere down there. This one drove a Corvette and wore Italian suits around the bait shop.

Sandra's small role, as far as Jack could remember, was that of a been-around-the-block cocktail waitress who cracked wise with the hero and presented herself as an open invitation.

Each show ended the same way. Sandra let Stryker Double know he could take her home that night, and the star got a look on his face as if to say hey, a guy could do worse. Cue theme music and roll credits.

Now Jack stared at the photograph on the seat next to him. He was sitting in his 1991 white Chevy Caprice, an ex–police cruiser that he had picked up at a city auction. The car was parked outside an Inwood Road hair salon and spa called Rodolfo's. Sherri had told him he could pick up the chase here. Sandra was getting a facial, Sherri said, and having her nails done.

It was just after two on a May afternoon. Sunny, with a stiff, unrefreshing breeze from the south. A little warm for camping in the car, but not bad if you found a shady spot. Dallas was still a month away from being unbearable.

Jack listened to the ball game on the radio and thought about his talk that morning with Sherri, who had counted on her fingers the strange calls, threatening messages, and possible stalkings that Sandra had told her about.

"She talked about a couple of heavy-breathing bits on the phone," Sherri had said. "Saw shadows outside the windows at night. I looked, baby, and I didn't see a thing. . . . Said she had a feeling that somebody was following her . . . And some notes on her windshield that said something like, 'I'll get you.'"

"You see these notes?" Jack had asked. "You still have them?"

"Exactly what I'm talking about, baby." Sherri shook her head and stared at the red rug. "I haven't seen a thing. That's the reason I called you."

Rodolfo's salon had cream stucco walls with white Greek-temple columns flanking the door. No name out front, just a large brass plaque with a simple *R* at its center. Jack sat in his car and watched an erratic parade of rich ladies come and go. They went in looking like a million bucks and came out looking like a couple more.

His own hair was cut at Casa View Barbers by a fat man named Vernell who listened to Rush Limbaugh and always had a cherry-flavored cough drop going. The last time Jack had been in the chair Vernell told him, "Getting a little thin back here on the crown."

"Jesus, what?" Jack had said, pressing his hand to the back of his head. His body was finally starting to fade on him. Just another reminder that he was all of thirty-five, cresting the actuarial hill. Wouldn't be long—ten years, twenty?—before his memory would start curling at the edges like old wallpaper. A few more sunrises and sunsets, that's all it would take. He didn't need much imagination to gaze a little further down the road and see a nursing home attendant cutting his meat for him.

Some men, reaching this gateway to middle age, fell apart. They ran around on their wives, they took stupid risks, they dumped their careers, they rocketed their lives into strange orbits. Not Jack. He'd already done all that, years ago.

Now Jack shifted in the car seat, pulled a comb from his back pocket, gave his head a couple of quick swipes, and counted the blond hairs jumping ship. He was up to seven or eight when the door to Rodolfo's opened and Sandra walked out.

He raised his binoculars to watch her. She wore a factory worker's sleeveless white t-shirt, tight faded jeans, and black knee-length boots. Barely five feet tall, he'd guess, but a body that could have come from the starlet factory.

She glided to a forest-green Mustang convertible, top down. Quick check of her hair in the mirror, sunglasses on, then she started the car, gunned it across the parking lot, and pulled into traffic without stopping. Jack had to scramble to keep up.

The Mustang turned left on Preston and headed north. Jack stayed back but kept her in sight. Reminding himself, he wasn't just following someone. He was following someone who maybe was being followed by someone else.

Just before Preston and Park he pushed an Al Green cassette into his player and looked up to see a furniture truck pulling into his lane. A van to his left kept him from going that way, and an old man in a Lincoln boxed him on the right. Everybody stopped; the light was red. By the time he cleared himself from the jam the green Mustang was out of sight.

Jack drove fifty-five when he could and busted two red lights, going three or four miles but not finding her. He turned around and backtracked a couple of miles, ready to kick himself and give up when he saw the Mustang in front of a 7-Eleven. A little closer and he made Sandra, in plain sight, talking on a pay phone and facing the street. Al Green was singing "Let's Stay Together."

She talked for a few more minutes. Then she was back in the Mustang, racing up Preston again, Jack struggling to stay with her as the neat grids of leafy residential streets flew past. After a left turn, Jack pulled a number from his pocket and dialed his car phone. Sherri Plunkett answered, and Jack said it looked as if Sandra was headed home.

"She likes to take herself a beauty sleep most afternoons," Sherri said.

Jack watched from the end of the block as the Mustang vanished into Sherri's driveway. "How long's she going to be at home?" he asked. It wasn't the kind of neighborhood where you could park on the street and sit unnoticed. "This could be a problem."

"Tell you what," Sherri said. "The people across from us has gone to Yurp."

Jack wanted to ask her, The hell are you talking about? But he said, "That's nice."

"Baby, Sherri's not telling you that 'cause it's nice. I'm saying they ain't home. They're in France."

"They went to Europe."

"That's what Sherri just said. Now listen. It's the two-story house directly across the street, the one with the two cement lions by the front door. You can hide out there."

The house with the lions had big trees and a thick hedge out front to give him some cover. He backed into the driveway, far enough in that he could see Sherri's house but not too obvious from the street. Then he waited in his car. He checked his messages and made some calls. He listened to the radio and, later, to his stomach growl. When he had to piss he went behind a hedge. By eight it was dark.

The lights came on upstairs at Sherri Plunkett's house, but the curtains stayed open. Jack could see Sandra move back and forth in a second-floor bedroom, taking clothes from a closet and laying them on a bed. After a few minutes she paused in front of the window, her back to him, and pulled her shirt off over her head. She turned to the side, unsnapped her jeans, and pushed them down with a shimmy of her hips.

Jack raised the binoculars and watched as Sandra did several minutes of stretching exercises. She reached for the ceiling, then touched her toes, at least twenty-five reps, all in front of the window. As far as Jack could tell, she was in good shape.

What she wasn't, was scared. Nobody afraid of a stalker pranced around in her underwear with the curtains open. That was the act of someone who wanted attention. Well, Jack thought as he kept the binoculars up, she had his.

Sandra Danielle and the green Mustang convertible, top down, left the driveway two hours later, going slowly this time. Jack followed with his lights off until the Mustang hit some traffic. He stayed with her south on the tollway and through downtown, all the way to Deep Ellum.

This used to be a part of town where you could find a pretty good selection of plumbing supplies, machine parts, and cheap rooms among the old red-brick buildings. The Aadams, a whorehouse-turned-flophouse, had been here. So had the Ship's

Anchor, a tavern for working stiffs. Eldon Earthman's used car lot, full of Detroit iron, had nailed down one corner. All vanished when the galleries, the precious bars, and the music clubs for people with nose rings moved in.

Sandra parked at a metered spot on Main, in front of a coffee place called Cuppa Joe. Same stuff you could get at Denny's but dressed up at five times the price, was the way Jack remembered it from his one visit. He drove past, made a U-turn at the end of the block, and pulled to the curb, watching as Sandra left her car and walked to Cuppa Joe's sidewalk tables. She had on a miniskirt and heels.

Jack got out of his Chevy in front of a restaurant that used to be called Eduardo's, until Eduardo went away for some elective surgery and returned as Monica. There were enough people going in and out of Monica's this time of night that Jack could lean against a light pole and not look like a purse snatcher in waiting.

Sandra had ordered something that came in a tall glass. She sipped her drink and seemed to watch the traffic without a lot of interest. A couple of times she checked her watch. After about ten minutes she paid for her drink and walked back to her car.

Jack wondered where they would be off to now. He moved to his car but didn't get in, waiting while Sandra paused outside the Mustang. She pulled something from her purse and held it in front of her face. Probably her keys, but hard to tell from a block away at night.

She leaned into the car, with the door closed and her miniskirt riding way up. Jack guessed she was putting the keys in the ignition. He couldn't understand why she stayed outside the Mustang. She might have been waiting for the passing traffic to clear before opening the door, but right now a red light down the street kept the block empty.

Maybe, he thought, she was just showing off her legs and her ass. Maybe this was someone who always wanted someone watching her. And if no one actually was watching, she could make someone up.

He was about to turn toward his own car when his eye picked up movement down the block. A man in dark clothes and a baseball cap walked into the street. Closer to Sandra he began to run.

She was opening the driver's-side door as the man reached her. There was a quick struggle and he pushed her into the car, then jumped in after her.

Jack sprinted up the street toward the Mustang but stopped when he saw that it was coming at him. It wasn't moving fast, but it was weaving some. The driver seemed to be trying to push Sandra's head down and steer the Mustang at the same time.

For a second or two Jack thought he would have to leap out of the way or get hit. He could see himself sprawled across the hood, hanging on to a windshield wiper as the driver swerved wildly and tried to shake him off. It happened to Stryker Double one time when he watched.

But the Mustang veered as it came closer, straddling the center line, and picked up a little speed. Jack turned, ready to run to his own car and give chase. It was blocked by a cab taking on passengers. He whirled back toward the Mustang just before it passed him.

If he'd had time to think it over, it occurred to him later, he might have done something different, though he wasn't sure what. He didn't run from fights, but he'd finessed his way around them plenty of times. Jack had always been someone to use his head before his fists. But all this worry lately about age, about his body in a slow decline, was messing with his thoughts, making caution seem like a weakness, growing doubts like weeds.

Jack took three running steps and dove toward the moving Mustang convertible.

He landed with his shoulder on the back seat, his head near the floorboard and his feet in the air. Jack heard the driver yell, "Shit!" The car braked, jerked to the right, and crashed into something, throwing Jack against the back of the front seats. Sandra shouted, "Ow!" and "Jesus, what are you doing?"

Jack scrambled up. The driver opened his door, on the way out. Jack reached over the front seat and locked an arm across the man's neck.

He wore a nylon stocking pulled over his head. The collar of his black turtleneck shirt had been pulled over his chin and mouth, Bazooka Joe style. Jack was surprised at how little he struggled. All the guy did was put his hand between his legs, then strike Jack once in the upper arm.

Jack didn't see the knife until it was sticking in him. It was in that patch of arm muscle just below the shoulder where they gave him his flu shots, and it caused a nasty sting over a deep, searing burn. Jack made a noise he'd never heard from himself before and fell against the back seat. Sandra shouted something he couldn't make out. The man jumped from the car, ran to the sidewalk, and disappeared around a corner.

The knife was sunk halfway to its brown wooden handle. Jack reached with his left hand and pulled it out with a quick and smooth stroke. It looked like something to slice tomatoes with. He put the knife on the seat beside him and pulled at the hole in his shirt, ripping away the sleeve to get a look at the wound.

"Oh, man, he popped you a good one, didn't he?" Sandra was still in the front seat, holding her hand to the side of her head. "How does it feel?"

"It hurts."

"Here." She opened the glove box and came back with a white hand towel. "Here you go."

The Mustang's front bumper was in a mangled kiss with the fender of a parked Jeep Cherokee. Three or four cars had come up in the lane behind them. One of the drivers hit his horn. Sandra stood in her seat and yelled, "Fuck off!" Then, to Jack, "You think you're okay?"

Jack pressed the towel against the wound. "I'm all right. How about you?"

She took her hand from her temple and checked her palm. "I got a whack to the head. But, hey, I'm great now that that maniac's gone."

Another of the stacked-up drivers blew his horn. Sandra yelled, "Go around, asshole!" She was giving him the finger when a police car made the corner.

They sat in the back of the patrol car, with Sandra Danielle giving Corporal J. G. Byers her account. The man came out of nowhere, she said. He put a knife to her throat and said, Get in, bitch.

"I thought I was *dead*," Sandra told Corporal Byers, a catch in her voice before she said *dead*, then a shiver to follow up. "I was so scared. I tried to scream and nothing, I mean not a thing, would come out. It was like my brain would not connect to my voice. Has that ever happened to you?"

"Not really," Corporal Byers said.

"I mean, the circuits just shut down. It was so weird. The power was off, you know what I mean?"

Another police car rolled up, and Corporal Byers gave the two cops in it a description of the suspect. They roared off after him in the general direction he had fled. Look for a guy, Jack thought, who's stupid enough to be walking around with a nylon over his head five minutes after running from a crime scene.

Corporal Byers put in a second call for an EMS crew to tend to Jack's wound. "They'll be right along," he said, then left his car to put some pink road flares alongside and behind the Mustang.

Jack pressed the towel against his shoulder and listened to the police radio. It was a busy night—a four-vehicle wreck on North Central, a nasty domestic on Gaston, a naked man sitting on a bench along Live Oak, someone with a gun barricaded in a house on Fitzhugh.

He stared straight ahead as Sandra turned to him. She said, "You were wonderful. I mean it, you were *great*. You didn't have to do that."

"That's not exactly true."

"The way you just came out of nowhere, it was like a script. I don't know you, I don't even know your name, and you just pop up to save my life. Like my own personal angel, you know?"

She leaned toward him. Jack thought she was going to give her angel a nice little kiss on the cheek to say thanks. He thought that until she put her hand on the inside of his thigh and licked his ear.

# 3

"You work this scam right, you can clear ten grand easy inna week," Teddy Tunstra II said. "All you need is—man, it reeks in here. You smell what I'm talking about, Mertts?"

"Don't smell a thing, Deuce."

"Fucking pine scent deodorizer." Teddy looked around the room, a hotel bar called Jingles on the north side of Houston, near the airport. The place was less than half full with some lonely secretaries and a few traveling salesmen in department store suits. Old farts' rock came over the sound system.

"What I'm telling you," Teddy said above the music, "is they don't shampoo the carpet. They just spray it wit that pine scent shit. Like nobody's gonna notice."

Mertts glanced toward the door. "You really believe the boy's gonna show?"

"Who, Duff?" Teddy said. Thinking, the fuck kind of name is that, anyway? Hey, a dog, sure. But a human?

Teddy had met Duff poolside at the hotel the day before, while Mertts was sleeping. They had a couple of drinks in the smoggy Gulf Coast evening, the sun an orange lozenge sinking in ooze. Duff, who said he'd come by the hotel for a nooner and stayed all day, was looking for opportunities. Teddy told him about his plan, and Duff said he'd be back the next day with some cash.

15

"Eleven-thirty sharp is what we agreed on," Teddy said, looking at the clock above the Jingles cash register. Duff was half an hour late. "Ten more minutes is all he gets from me, on account udda stench innis dump."

"Whatever you say, Deuce," Mertts said.

Teddy smelled beer, smoke, sweat, popcorn, urinal cakes, margarita mix, and breath mints. Somebody nearby was wearing Brut. Ever since the fight, when the tip of his nose got twisted and bent, his sense of smell acted as if it were turbocharged. He caught a whiff of some perfume like candy. It took Teddy back to a corner bodega in his old neighborhood, Astoria, Queens. Happy memories: He had shoplifted that store bare.

"You want another brew?" Mertts leaned both elbows on the bar and rubbed with thick fingers above his left temple, massaging a big L-shaped scar. He signaled to the bartender with his other hand.

"He's gonna stand us up? This Duff? Fuck him." Teddy admired himself in the mirror behind the bar. His cream-colored silk jacket had a nice drape to it, thanks to the bulking up Teddy had done during his time out of circulation. His dark hair was perfect as usual. "You and me can pull it off ourselves, Mertts. All we gotta do is get the up-front cash somewhere else. We do that, we clear ten grand inna week, easy, you and me. Fifteen, we hustle it hard."

"Talking the talk now, Deuce." Mertts pulled a snuff tin from the back pocket of his jeans, opened it on the bar, and took two tablets from it. A couple dozen remained. "But how's it supposed to work again?"

Teddy looked at Mertts: six-five, 350 pounds, with a steel plate in his head where a golf-loving homeowner, objecting to a midnight burglary, had buried a five iron in his skull. "Well," Teddy said, "like I told you a couple times before. We find a house for lease, a nice place inna suburbs. An effing showcase home, I'm talking about. Tree, four bedrooms, maybe even one wit a Jacuzzi love tub inna batroom."

Mertts placed the two tablets on his tongue and swallowed some beer. "Bud's good." He smiled. "But Bud and Talwin is better. . . . Go ahead, man, I'm listening."

"So we pay the first month's rent and take possession udda house," Teddy said, "which is where Duff's stake comes in. Then we advertise it inna paper, beautiful house for rent, owner transferred. Promise the place to any chump who can pay the first month and the deposit in cash. Phony up a lease. Maybe get ten or fifteen suckers to rent the place. Tell each of them they can move in next week."

"Next week."

"By which time, Mertts, me and you and all that cash has left town."

"Man, Deuce, I love to see your mind work."

A voice behind them said, "Teddy, my young friend."

Teddy turned to see a little rooster of a guy, early fifties, with a thin mustache and a comb-over. He wore a slick leather coat over a shirt unbuttoned to midchest, tight designer jeans, and alligator-skin loafers.

"Yo, Duff." Teddy shook his hand. "We was beginning to worry about you."

"Getting my ashes hauled." Duff winked. "Ran a little overtime."

"Hey, no problem," Teddy said. "You bring the stake?"

Duff shook his head and cupped an ear, saying over the music, "Did I what?"

Some Neil Diamond crap was blasting. *Cracklin' Rosie get on board . . .* With fat people on the dance floor. It made Teddy want to throw up. He said, "How about we go talk inna parking lot?"

It was a muggy night. The three of them crossed the asphalt lot and stopped at Duff's burgundy Jaguar. "So, Duff," Teddy said. "You brought the stake, am I right? Couple grand cash, I think was the word mentioned."

Mertts stood with his hands in his pockets, staring toward the freeway. Duff leaned across the hood of the Jag and brushed at something. The parking lot's lights reflected off the paint job. "Pretty nice set of wheels, wouldn't you say?"

"Not bad." Teddy bent to look inside but couldn't see through the smoked-glass windows. "Hey, we got a deal or what?"

"They don't give you a car like this for being stupid," Duff said. "People who drive cars like this got something on the ball."

Teddy straightened and faced him. "Meaning what?"

"This house you want to rent out, tell me about it." Duff moved to the front, where he picked dead bugs off the grille. "Where is it, what's it look like?"

"Hey, it's got a roof, some windows, a couple doors. The fuck should I know? We ain't found it yet."

Duff laughed. "You're joking. You're pulling Duff Harvey's leg."

Teddy sniffed, looked away, then came back to Duff. "The fuck's happening here? You said you'd bring the stake. You doing a crabwalk on me now?"

Duff took a handkerchief from his jacket and began to polish the front bumper. "Teddy, my friend, cool down. I'm just doing some due diligence here. I'm reading the prospectus, you might say."

"I might say, but I dint."

"I was under the impression when we talked yesterday"— Duff stood and wiped off the hood ornament—"that this whole deal was a bit more than pie in the sky."

Mertts had come over to join them, yawning and rubbing the side of his head.

Duff didn't look up from his shine job. "So now you're saying what? That Duff Harvey's supposed to buy a cat in a sack?"

Teddy blew some air and shook his head. "You're so fucking smart, Duff? Tell me how we was supposed to go out and rent this house wit no stake?"

Duff stood and checked his watch. "I gotta make tracks. What say we get together on this later."

"We had an arrangement," Teddy said.

"Hey, gents, I don't even know you two. All right? You, Teddy, I just met yesterday. And you"—Duff turned and looked up at Mertts—"all I know about you is you're damn big. I don't even know your name."

"Fredrick Mertts."

Duff smiled. "Your name's Fred Mertts?"

"No, motherfucker, it's Fred*rick*."

"You banged Ethel lately?" Duff laughed. "Hey, Fred Mertts. I think Lucy's on the phone. Ricky Ricardo needs some help with his bongo drums."

Teddy watched it happen, didn't try to stop the show. If Duff was going to weasel, he deserved what he got. Which was Mertts's fist, a big overhand right, crashing onto the top of the little man's head.

Duff dropped to the black pavement, out cold. Mertts kicked him twice in the face. Saying, "Make fun of *my* name?"

Teddy stepped around Mertts and took Duff's wallet and keys from the pockets of the designer jeans. He got in the Jag, started it, and rolled the window down. Mertts was giving Duff another kick. Teddy said, "I don't think he'll make fun no more. Let's go."

They swung by their car, another stolen job but with nowhere near the class of a Jag, and grabbed their suitcases. Then Teddy gassed it.

Three or four miles down the road, when he was sure nobody was following, Teddy pulled over. He got a moist towelette package from his jacket, tore open the envelope, and wiped down the steering wheel. Telling Mertts, "Hey, who knows where the guy's hands been." The smell of alcohol and peppermint filled the car.

Mertts was sweating and still breathing hard. He dried his face with his sleeve. "Sorry I lost it, man. But the little mother cheesed me off."

"He shoulda known better than to crabwalk on Teddy Deuce." Teddy took Duff's wallet from the space between the seats. "See what he's got innere—holy shit, check this, Mertts."

Teddy pulled money from the wallet and began to count out loud. "Two grand in big bills, six hundred in change," he said when he was done. "Plus an American Express, a Diner's Club, and a Visa Gold."

"Them's sweet sounds, Deuce. Almost like a song, you know it?" The two of them stared at the money until Mertts said, "So what do we do now?"

Teddy folded the bills back in the wallet. He thought for a few seconds. Then, "Got tree hundred miles of driving ahead of us."

"That gives me plenty of time for a nap."

"'Cause there's a guy I wanna see"—Teddy shifted the Jag into drive—"in Dallas."

"All right, Big D," Mertts said. "Point the way, Deuce."

# 4

He was still sore from the dude grabbing him. Dean Dudley sat at a table in Butch & Madman's Saloon and Grubhouse, a sports bar in a prefab warehouse, northwest Dallas. At nine in the morning the place was nearly empty.

Dean ran his eyes over the idle video games and looked at all the junk—antique tricycles, brass horns, autographed baseball bats—that decorated the walls. He rubbed the front of his neck. Thinking, it was attack of the crazy man last night from this dude who thinks he's Superman. Who believes he's one of the X-Men. Who's so nuts he jumps into a moving car.

Dean got hot all over again at the thought of the guy diving into the Mustang and wrapping his arm around Dean's throat. Next time, he told himself, I'll have a bigger blade. Next time, a butcher knife. To teach Captain Flying Dickhead some respect for Dean Dudley.

As if Dean didn't have enough to worry about already. He gazed across some pool tables to see Ricks Harrison at the bar, on the phone. When their eyes met, Ricks gave Dean a two-fingered wave and kept talking. Dean turned away and muttered, "Asshole."

Two minutes later he looked up to see Ricks standing beside his table. "Mind if I sit down?" Ricks said. Dean thought, You call me on the phone, you say to get my butt down here if I know what's good for me, you treat me like a piece of garbage, and now you want to know do I mind if you sit down? Biggest flaming jerk in town, this dude.

"Hey," Dean said, "be my guest."

Ricks wore a pressed button-down shirt, white, with a white monogram on the cuff. Dean looked at the thin gold bracelet peeking from beneath his sleeve and the gold ring dangling from his left earlobe. Hair was thick brown and swept back, every bit of it in place. Ricks smelled like the men's cologne counter at Neiman's. And he acts, Dean thought, he acts like he's doing the world a favor just by walking on it.

"Oh, my, Dinky," Ricks said as he took his chair. He shook his head slowly. "Dinky, Dinky, Dinky."

"The name's Dean. You're gonna talk to me, Ricks, use my name, okay? Could you do that for me, man?"

"You know, Dinky, I thought you were going to pull it off. I'm watching the game last night, Rockets have the Mavericks by fifteen with, what, thirty seconds to play? And I said to myself, how about that, Dinky's finally clawed his way back. I'm thinking, it must be true what they say, every dog does have his day. You know?"

Dean looked at the floor.

"But let's go to the videotape," Ricks said.

"Don't, man." Dean shook his head. "Don't give me the play-by-play. The last thing I want to—"

"Jackson hits a three." Ricks held an imaginary microphone in front of his face. "Mavericks down by twelve with fifteen to play. Rockets inbound, bring it down and turn it over. Jason Kidd, with a who-gives-a-shit heave from half-court, drains another three at the buzzer. Yes! Rockets by nine. Do you believe in miracles?" Ricks smoothed his hair and dropped his voice. "Point spread, if you'll recall, Dinky, was nine and a half."

"I want to double down tonight," Dean said. "I'll take the Pacers plus seven against the Knicks. Ewing's got a sore knee."

Ricks put two slim fingers into the pocket of his shirt and came back with an index card. He studied the figures on it, then waved it slowly in front of Dean. "Little Mister Card says Dinky's ten thousand and change on the short side."

"Hey, man, I know that. I can count, you know. I can add up numbers." Dean felt as if his head were about to blow. "I'm taking the double down on the Pacers-Knicks, all right? Are we through now? 'Cause I gotta go."

Ricks slid the card back in his pocket. "I don't think the man I work for will allow you any more extensions."

The room seemed to whirl around Dean. "I don't see"—his voice rose higher—"I don't see what the problem is, Ricks."

"Easy, Dinky. Down, boy." Ricks smiled. Every word arrived encased in its own cube of ice. "Of course we'll have to insist on full payment of balance due."

Dean's throat was hurting now as if Captain Flying Dickhead had the squeeze on it again. "Hey, Ricks, I'm good for it. You know that. I got money coming, Ricks, just as soon as—"

"Then there's no problem. We'll take payment now, thank you."

"Who hangs with ten thousand in their pocket, Ricks? Richest dude in the world, he walked in here right now, he wouldn't have that kind of stash on him. Give me time to pull it together, how about."

Ricks stood. "Noon Monday, big Dink. Final offer." He snapped his fingers and pointed with both hands. "See you then."

"Monday?" Dean's breaths came one on top of the other. "What's Monday, man? It's just a day on the calendar. Why you picking Monday, Ricks? I mean, Wednesday's a good day. Wednesday, Thursday—nothing wrong with those days. They're good days, Ricks."

Ricks leaned forward, hands flat on the table. "I know all about you, all right? I know your setup. What I don't understand?

I don't understand why Dinky's supposed to be a rich man but cries like a poor one."

Because that's the way it is, Dean thought as he watched Ricks walk away. But, he told himself, things could change. Could? Shit, they had to.

It looked like a poorly maintained rural route—badly paved, uncurbed, with open ditches running along each side. A road where you wouldn't be surprised to see an old pickup toting hay, or a rusting Pontiac en route to the trailer park.

Actually, Strait Lane ran right through the big-money heart of North Dallas. It was flanked by sprawling showcase houses set well back from the street on manicured acreage: country estates for people who didn't want to leave the city.

Split-rail fences bordered bogus pastures that never saw a cow. There were tennis courts where barns would be. No stock tanks, but almost every house had a big pool.

Jack's Chevy Caprice bounced over Strait Lane's holes and bad patch jobs. This quaint touch of rural life, he told himself, was about as real as the Western getups the society matrons wore at the Cattle Baron's Ball. If they wanted, people in these houses could be on the phone to the mayor in the morning and have a city crew paving the street with emeralds that afternoon.

Several men with mowers trimmed the lawn as Jack pulled into the sweeping greystone driveway in front of Sherri's place. The house was a two-story train wreck of styles: Southwestern limestone exterior, odd contemporary angles, and white columns that could have been trucked in from a Mississippi plantation. One section, a single-floor graft onto the side, had a roof that rose in a rounded swelling. Sherri had told him her late husband Omer designed the place. Call it, Jack thought as he parked his car, the Omerdome.

Sherri opened the front door before he could ring the

chimes. "How you feeling, baby?" she asked. "Your shoulder okay? Tell Sherri if you're doing all right."

Jack waited until she sat down, then took his own seat. They were in the red room. "If I had to get stabbed"—Jack pointed to his shoulder—"that was the place to do it. So the doc said, anyway."

"I just couldn't believe it." Sherri put a drink on the table beside her. "Sandra woke me up when she came home last night and told me the whole story. I thought I was having a nightmare with my eyes open. I did. Just thinking about that crazy nut with a knife—that had me shaking, hon, like a whore in church."

"When you phoned this morning—"

"Sandra told me, Don't call him too early, the boy had a rough night. I asked her how the hell she thought I slept, after what happened." Sherri sipped her drink. "I think Sandra likes you."

Just past noon, and Sherri was still in her robe, a cranberry-colored silk number that was a little too loosely tied, it seemed to Jack. Her hair and makeup were fixed, though. Jack wore an old pair of jeans, black cowboy boots, and his last clean white shirt. His back was sore from the leap into the Mustang. His right shoulder still hurt from the knife, and his left one from the tetanus shot.

"I didn't expect to hear from you," he said.

"Woke you up, you mean? Coulda fooled Sherri. You sounded clear as a bell. Good Lord, where's my manners? How about a cocktail?"

Jack shook his head. "I didn't expect to hear from you because I didn't figure I'd be working for you anymore. I think you need more than what I've got to offer."

Sherri finished her drink and rattled the ice in her glass. "Let's go freshen this up."

He followed her out of the red room and into a sunken living area with a high, round ceiling—the underside of the dome.

It had fluffy white carpet and white furniture with mirrored walls. The fixtures were chrome and glass. Over the white brick fireplace hung another six-foot portrait, this one of a smiling man standing on skis in snow. He cradled a rifle with the barrel down, and wore a fur-lined white parka and a gray Stetson. In the painting's background was a dead polar bear, blood draining from its mouth.

"Quite a place," Jack said.

Sherri pulled on one of the tall mirrored panels. It opened to reveal a bar. "Omer called this one the North Pole Room." She broke the seal on a bottle of vodka. "Had special air condition-ing installed so it'd stay extra-cool in here no matter what the weather was. Hundred and ten degrees outside, Omer'd come in here and make a fire." Sherri poured vodka and tomato juice in her glass, then glanced toward the ceiling. "There's a fan at the top of the chimney so it'll draw in the summertime."

Jack pointed to the portrait. "I'm guessing that's Omer."

Sherri took a sip of her drink, smacked her lips, and gazed at the picture. "Now who else would it be, baby?"

Jack studied Omer's round nose, weak chin, and big ears. "Sandra doesn't look much like him."

"And thank the Lord for that." Sherri shut the mirrored door to the bar. "Now, where were we? Has Sherri made you an offer yet?"

Jack sat on a white couch. "You said on the phone you want-ed to . . . how'd you put it? Saddle me up for the big rodeo."

"Well, there you go. Make everybody happy and say yes." She dropped into a large chair and sloshed some of the drink on her robe as she landed. When she crossed her legs Jack looked away.

"You know," he said, "if there's a guy trying to grab your daughter off the streets, I think you might want to bring in reinforcements. Extra security."

"That's why Sherri called you, baby."

"Protection's not my deal." Jack left the couch and walked to a window. "I don't carry a gun, and I'm just one guy. I poke around, I don't protect. I snoop."

"Fifteen hundred dollars a day," Sherri said.

Jack stood at the window and parted the curtains. The room looked out onto a large Texas-shaped swimming pool. He turned to Sherri. "Have the police called Sandra today? A Detective Ramirez from Crimes Against Persons? He phoned me this morning right after you did, asking questions about last night. Said he was going to call Sandra, too."

"Fifteen hundred dollars a day." Sherri swirled her ice with her finger. "Find out who's after my Sandra, that's what I want. Find out who this crazy man is."

Jack looked out the window once more, to the far end of the pool, near the Panhandle. Sandra lay on a chaise longue, on her stomach, one knee bent with her foot in the air, sunbathing nude. Sherri said, "What the hell, two thousand a day. How's that? I think Sherri's talking your tongue now, baby. Two thousand a day, that'll make just about anybody's head nod up and down."

The bags lay on Dean's back seat, tools and equipment from Sears and Wald's Police Supply. Atop the car, tied down with rope, was a sheet of half-inch plywood.

Dean drove his arctic-silver BMW 740i, a wedding present from his new bride, west on Commerce Street. He went past the county jail and over the old bridge crossing the Trinity. Spring rains had the river running the color of dirty chocolate milk. Dean turned up the radio and listened to a country song about a loving, devoted wife. He talked back to the singer, saying, "You oughtta meet mine, asshole."

The BMW, with the Dallas skyline in its rearview mirror, came off the bridge and followed the wide road past a weedy stretch of vacant lots, bail bonding agencies, and heavy equipment yards. After a mile or so Dean took the fork onto Fort Worth Avenue.

This used to be a highway for happy motoring, the best way to head west out of Dallas back when they made cars with fins. If you needed a place to sleep, eat, or gas up, Fort Worth Avenue had it.

That was before the state built the turnpike. Now Fort Worth Avenue was a six-lane, potholed back alley where Echeverria's Used Tires did slow business next to Maria's Tarot Parlor, just around the curve from an overgrown graveyard with an unmarked plot holding the bones of Clyde Barrow.

Still scattered along the roadside were the remains of half a dozen old tourist courts. Some had boards over their windows and were surrounded by chain link topped with barbed wire. Others managed to stay in business by renting rooms to day laborers, hookers, and travelers without the scratch for a Motel 6.

The Texan Trail Motor Inn was a semicircle of twelve detached units, half of them still usable. Each had a midget Alamo facade, covered with mildewed white stucco that looked like mayonnaise gone bad. With a landscape of untended yucca plants and spindly mimosa trees, the Texan spread across the side of what passed for a hill in Dallas. The cracked asphalt parking lot had three cars and one dog in it when Dean pulled in.

Dean downshifted the BMW and steered uphill past the twelve Alamos. He followed the pavement to a bumpy, narrow road that curved behind the motel units and led to a stuccoed box of a building.

The building had four apartments, two upstairs and two down. That morning, Dean had rented all four for a week. Five hundred dollars total, paid to a greasy clerk in a torn polyester shirt behind the desk in the Texan Trail office.

Now Dean parked his car, took the bags from the back seat, and climbed rickety wooden stairs to apartment 4. He had picked number 4 because it was the only one whose smell didn't make him gag. "Exterminator man put some poison out couple a weeks ago," the clerk had explained. "Some squirrels mighta died in the walls."

Apartment 4 was a one-bedroom unit with a faded pink paint job and a green linoleum floor. It had a wood-grain plastic-veneer dresser, a chrome-and-Formica table with two chairs, and a tartan convertible couch.

Dean put the bags on the table and walked to the back window, where he gazed over a large field of tall grass and scrub hackberries. The brush almost hid six or eight rusted car bodies and a dozen abandoned refrigerators: metal carcasses upside down or on their sides, doors hanging open, scattered across the field as if the cars and refrigerators had fought a battle and left their dead.

Dean drew a plastic shade the color of old newspaper over the window and turned on the overhead light. He began to unpack the bags: bolts and screws, wrenches and screwdrivers, shop rags and bolt cutters, a Polaroid camera, and all the rest.

When he was done he went to the front door, stepped onto the porch, and looked across the empty, unpaved lot. He'd been given a new day, and had a new plan.

But, he wondered with a glance back at the bedroom, would four sets of handcuffs and ten feet of chain be enough?

# 5
## 2

*J*ack and Sherri walked in the early afternoon sun along the Rio Grande side of the Texas-shaped pool. Sandra sat up on her chaise longue and pulled a towel around herself.

"Good news," Sherri said, looking at Sandra. "Your angel's done flapped his wings and flown home. He's hired on."

"Angel for Hire." Sandra stood. "Sounds like a show on Fox." Jack watched her rise and walk toward a bathhouse on the north side of the pool, where Oklahoma would be. Just before she reached the door she glanced back and said, "Be right there." The towel fell open, giving Jack a flash of a view. She turned and walked inside.

Sherri took a pair of sunglasses from the pocket of her robe. "Told you she likes you."

Jack squinted into the light reflecting off the windblown pool, like gold scales on the water. He asked, "Did Sandra get along with Omer?"

Sherri didn't answer right away, settling into a chair next to a round white table shaded by an open umbrella. Finally she said, "What do you think I'm thinking about?" She rattled the ice in her glass.

"Wild guess? Another drink."

"I'm just trying to imagine what it woulda been like around here if Omer and Sandra had ever lived under the same roof."

Sherri shook her head. "Wouldn't be no zipper made that could hold Omer then."

"Sherri, you know what I like?" Jack took the chair next to her. "I like stories with a beginning, a middle, and an end, in that order. Let's hear yours."

"My story." Sherri turned her dark glasses his way. "Now that would take a whole lotta time."

"No problem with that," Jack said. Thinking, When you're making two grand a day, time is something you have plenty of. "I'm ready to listen."

The door to the bathhouse opened, and Sandra came out in black boxer shorts and a sleeveless ribbed shirt. "Here's what I can't forget," Sherri said, pointing a polished red nail at Sandra. "The second time I set my eyes on this little girl right here."

Sandra pulled her chair close to Jack, dropped into it, and said, "Tell me again." She rested her hand on Jack's arm. "Tell both of us. What went through your mind when you saw me?"

"Okay." Sherri took a pack of Salem Lights and a lighter from a pocket of her robe. "Tell you a story. Two weeks ago the doorbell rings. I was expecting a package from UPS, some make-up I'd ordered, Sun King cosmetics—"

"Oh, that's the best stuff," Sandra said.

"So I go to the door and open it. I don't even look out the peephole, I just open it right up, and guess who's standing there." She reached under table and tapped Jack on the knee. "Go ahead, baby, guess. Who's standing there?"

"The UPS man," Jack said.

Sherri and Sandra laughed together. Jack looked from one face to the next, searching for resemblance. "Remember what you said?" Sherri to Sandra. "Tell him, go ahead."

"What a trip." Sandra shook her hair. "She opened the door and I looked her up and down. Just taking her in, you know. Then I'm like, 'Hi, Mom, it's me. I've come home, all grown up.'"

"Ain't that the truth." Sherri threw her head back and

laughed some more. Sandra stared at Jack. He stared back. She had green eyes with blades of light brown, like grass cut yesterday. Her nipples tried to poke their way through her thin shirt.

"Why'd you come home?" Jack asked Sandra. "The convent go on spring break?"

"Tell you what," Sherri said, "that just about floored me, that word *Mom*." She lit her cigarette. "That was a first for Sherri, better believe that. Mom. Talk about a word that comes out and kicks your butt to the corner and back."

Jack shook his head. "The more you two talk, the less I understand."

"What's to understand?" Sherri lowered her sunglasses and looked at Jack. "Nineteen sixty-two, an unmarried young lady named Sherri LeBonne—I'm talking about me, baby—has a little girl and gives her up for adoption. Never holds the child, walks out of Parkland Hospital with empty arms. Sad story, right? Breaks your heart, okay? But thirty-four years later, the doorbell rings and this beautiful woman here says, 'Hi, Mom.'" Sherri put her sunglasses back in place. "Now who says life ain't one strange thing after another?"

"Not me," Jack said. He turned to Sandra.

"My turn?" She folded her hands in front of her and talked like a schoolgirl giving a speech. "My life, by Sandra Danielle. I was adopted and raised by a wonderful couple in Orange County, California, Harry and Ellen. Ellen passed away last year."

"Cancer," Sherri said, breathing smoke. "That's what you said, right? Ate up with it at the end."

Sandra nodded. "They had her funeral in this beautiful church in Garden Grove, just awesome. Killer stained glass, you should have seen it. Big choir, lots of flowers. Hey, it was a production. Hard to believe it was real, you know?"

Sherri frowned. "Funerals wouldn't be so bad if they didn't always put a dead person at the front of the room."

Jack looked at Sandra. "So how did you get from there to here?"

Sandra tossed her hair again. "I've been on this show—"

"*Double or Nothing*," Sherri interrupted. "I told him all about it yesterday."

"We were between seasons. So I was sort of at loose ends for a few days. One morning I woke up and I thought, my mother. My real mother. I had an appointment for a seaweed wrap that afternoon, but all I could think about was one thing: I want to find my mother."

"That is out of this world," Sherri said, giving a smile full of wonderment.

"I paid a couple thousand dollars to a lawyer, he tracked the records down and"—Sandra beamed and opened her arms wide—"*ta-da*."

"Lemme ask you a question." Sherri leaned across the table toward Sandra. "And I want God's honest truth. All right?"

"Okay," Sandra said, not sounding sure.

"Here it is. No bullshit, now."

"Uh-huh?"

"Does he wear a rug?"

"Who?"

"The man on the show. Double."

"Eric? That's his real hair."

"Not Eric. Stryker."

Sandra shook her head, puzzled. "What are you talking about?"

"I'm talking about the roadkill the man on that TV program wears on his head."

Sandra sighed and cleared her throat. "The actor's name is Eric. His character's name is Stryker."

"Exactly what I said."

"And yes, that's his real hair."

Sherri sniffed and looked across the pool. "Looks fake to

Sherri." She turned to Jack and rattled the ice in her glass. "What about you, baby?"

"This is my own hair," he said. Thinking, What's left of it.

"That's not what I'm talking about." Sherri shook her glass again. "I'm asking do you want a cocktail." She didn't wait for an answer. "Let's have a round for everybody."

Sandra bounced from her chair. "I'll do it."

When she had gone into the house they listened to the birds singing and the wind in the oaks. After a minute or so Jack said, "All those years, you never heard from her?"

"Hell of a story, huh, baby?"

"Let me ask a rude question. How do you know she didn't come back just to get your money?" Sherri turned her sunglasses toward him. "Maybe," Jack said, "she heard about your financial condition and decided to get a piece of it. Have you thought about that?"

"You ever been rich?" Sherri looked at her rings. "I mean rolling-in-it rich."

"Not even close."

"First thing anybody with money finds out is how many hands there is in the world. And all of 'em stuck out and pointed your way, palm up. Cousins you never knew you had. Diseases you never heard of. Somebody called me on the phone the other day, wanted me to kick in for wart research. You think Sherri's joking?"

Jack waited while Sherri complained about investment scammers, sure-thing promoters, schools that wanted to build new gyms, churches that needed roof repairs, and every hard-luck case you could imagine. All of them were after her money. "Makes it so you don't even want to answer the phone. But . . ." She lit another cigarette and blew out the smoke. "Tell you what it does for you. Gives you a good nose. Know what Sherri means, baby? Pick up the scent a mile off."

The back door opened and Sandra came out carrying a tray

of glasses and bottles. "That little girl right there?" Sherri pointed. "She hasn't asked me for one red cent. Hell, I'm the one that talked her into moving in here. Right, hon? I kept after you to move in, didn't I?"

Sandra set the tray on the table. "Two days, that's all I planned to stay. Now here it is, two weeks." She walked to Sherri's chair and hugged her from behind. "Just me and my mom."

"This stalker," Jack said. "Maybe somebody who saw you on TV?"

Sandra released the hug and took her chair. "I thought about that."

"Besides the notes on your windshield, anyone sent you any strange letters? Or made weird calls?" Jack watched her shake her head. "Anybody acting obsessed?"

Sandra sipped from her glass. "I haven't had a letter or a call since I left L.A. I mean, nobody even knows I'm here."

"Somebody does," Jack said.

"Tell you what, it pisses Sherri off." Sherri pulled her robe tighter. Ragged fingers of the oaks' shadows had started to creep across the table. "Such a beautiful story, the way this little girl came home." She had a tremble in her voice. "That's the only word for it, baby, beautiful."

"It was like a force, you know?" Sandra stared across the pool. "I mean, there was just this voice telling me to come here."

"And now some crazy nut has to come in and mess everything up." Sherri dropped her cigarette butt into the melted ice of her old glass. It landed with a hiss. "I've wracked my brain night and day, and I don't know who it is. He could come walking up to me right now, I wouldn't know him from Adam's dog. But I do know this: If somebody screws with Sherri, Sherri screws back." She smiled Jack's way. "That's where you come in, baby."

Dean pulled his silver BMW 740i into the half-circle greystone driveway and entered the big house through the front door. It was quiet inside. He walked through the North Pole Room and into the kitchen, where he got himself a beer from the refrigerator. Four, five, six big swallows in a row hit the spot. Back at the KA house, nobody could chug beer like Dean. Fraternity champion, 1985 Spring Rush Chug-A-Thon.

When the bottle was empty he looked out the kitchen window and saw them sitting around a table poolside: Sherri, Sandra and—*whoa*—Captain Flying Dickhead. He had expected to see the dude again, just not quite so soon. Dean headed for the door to the pool area, glad he had worn his complete disguise when they first met. Telling himself, Watch how I handle the motherfucker this time.

But before he reached the door he made an about-face. With Sherri outside, he didn't want to waste an opportunity. Dean crossed back through the North Pole Room, climbed the curving staircase, and walked down the hall to Sherri's bedroom. To Sherri's shrine. Forty framed pictures and all of them of her.

He found her purse, a black shoulder bag with sequins, on a hook in the closet. Hanging there in the Sherri dress museum, a closet big as a garage, racks and racks of stuff she'd never even worn, price tags still dangling from a lot of it.

Dean had to claw through the scarves, brushes, lipstick tubes, matchbooks, and other junk in the purse before he found the money clip. Engraved gold, of course. He took folded bills from the clip and counted: $850 in all. A hundred and a few twenties went in his pocket—she'd never miss them—with the rest going back in the purse.

On the way out of the bedroom he stopped at her jewelry box, a big wooden job like a treasure chest with necklaces and bracelets spilling from it. He nabbed a pair of diamond earrings. Just an American boy building his fortune, he thought as he went downstairs, a couple of stones at a time.

He walked out the back door and toward the pool, waving

36

and talking, keeping an eye on Captain Flying Dickhead's face to make sure the dude didn't make him. Now that would be a nasty scene. "Hey, hey, hey," Dean said. "What have we got here? Looks like a family reunion. What's going on, kids? What a day for going poolside, huh? Sunshine big-time."

Sherri looked up and said, "What the hell you want?"

Dean gave her a smile. "Have no fear, Dean is here. How's everybody hanging this afternoon? We're all looking good, I can see that. We're all looking the best." Thinking, Except for you, you drunk old bag.

"Dean, this is Jack Flippo." Sherri pointed from one to the other. "He's doing some work for me."

"Hey, Jack," Dean said. "Totally good deal. What's up, Jack?" Dean walked to his side of the table as the guy stood. He was taller than Dean thought he would be, but skinny. Captain Flying Stringbean Dickhead.

The guy was giving him a hard look. "Hey, good to see you," Dean said. "Good to see anybody, that's what I say." Dean was ready to put his plan into action. He would shake the dude's hand and give him a big friendly hey-buddy whack on the shoulder, right in the same place he'd nailed him with the knife. Then watch the guy's face, see him shrivel up in pain, how funny would that be?

"Looks like we're all having a great time here today," Dean said. "Looks like we're all ready to get down and party hearty." He rolled his head back and bellowed, "Party!"

Then Dean grabbed Captain Dickhead's hand and squeezed hard. He was just about to smack the wounded shoulder when the thought hit him—*which one?* The guy had two shoulders, and Dean had stuck the knife in one of them while looking in the mirror, and things you saw in the mirror were backwards, so was it the right or the left? He'd had his back to the guy when he knifed him, but now they were facing each other, so would that cancel out the mirror making everything backward or would it

37

keep it backward because now he was turned around? Left or right? Right or left? Dean's mind whirled.

Jack heard the back door slam, and watched the man come across the pool patio toward the table. Early thirties, walking fast and working his mouth all the way. Saying, "Hey, y'all, what're you up to?" And, "Boys and girls, I think the party bell's rung."

Dean was about five-ten but muscular. Wide face, tiny nose, and small lizard eyes. High annoying voice that didn't quit, full of country twang. Wearing tight jeans, sneakers that probably cost a couple hundred, a green knit shirt, and a white golf visor.

He had yet to stop jabbering. Dean reminded Jack of an assistant he had worked with in the district attorney's office, Sparky Barker, fresh out of law school but knowing everything already and dying to tell everyone about it. Sparky never stopped talking. Even Johnny Hector, the DA, noticed. One day Johnny Hector told Sparky, "Son, if somebody sewed your lips shut you'd fart yourself to death."

Now Dean bounced around the table toward Jack, full of hey-how-you-doing as he came. Jack took a step to meet him. They shook hands and shook again, with Jack trying to take his hand back but Dean holding on tight. Jack watched Dean's eyes as they darted from Jack's left shoulder to his right.

Sherri lit her last cigarette, wadded up the empty package, and said, "Dean, go get me some smokes."

Jack pulled his hand free. Dean looked confused. He was still ping-ponging his gaze from one side of Jack to the other. His mouth was open, but for once nothing came out.

"You hear me, Dean?" Sherri's voice grew louder. "Go down to the minimart and get me some smokes. Some time today, how about."

Dean stood motionless until Sherri tossed the crumpled cigarette package at him and hit the side of his face. "What language is Sherri speaking?" she said. "The minimart. Now. Three packs of Salem Lights. Some lighter fluid, too. I'm running low. Anybody need anything else? Anybody? No? Dean, tell everbody goodbye now."

When he was gone, Sherri shook her head. "Harder to train than a goddamn circus poodle."

Jack pointed in the direction of Dean's exit. "Who exactly is that?"

Sherri blew a gray cloud and watched it float toward the ribs of the umbrella. "Dean?" she said. "Dean's my new husband."

# 6

It was dark, with heavy fog hanging, when Teddy Tunstra and Fredrick Mertts reached Dallas. Teddy drove Duff's Jag while Mertts slept.

Just past the city limits Mertts stirred, blinked, yawned, and stretched. "What a dream that was, Deuce." He snorted and wiped his nose with the back of his hand. "Mighta been the best one I ever had, I shit you not. Wanna hear about it?"

Teddy changed lanes and blew by three trucks in a row. He looked at Mertts. "Man, you're sweating like a pig."

"Set the scene for you." Mertts made a frame with his hands. "It's back in the old-timey days of the sailing ships. And the pirates is ripping everybody off. So the people come to me, 'cause I'm a captain. I say, all right, I'll go catch 'em. I head out in my own ship, and guess what happens."

"You turn into a pirate, too. The fucking meanest that ever lived."

"How the hell'd you know that? I mean how'd you—"

Teddy tapped the middle of the dashboard. "It was onna radio, Mertts. Paul Harvey, Rest Udda Story. You're dreaming while Paul Harvey's talking."

Mertts stared at Teddy, mouth open, then shook his head. "Too much."

"Hate to tell you," Teddy said, "but I think they strung you up in the end."

Mertts blew some air. They were quiet for a few minutes. Finally Teddy said, "Last time I was onnis road here, Mertts? My ass sat on a bus headed straight to Huntsville."

Mertts nodded slowly. "The highway to Fuck-you-up City. Couldn't sleep a wink myself."

"Man, the stench onnat bus."

"But look at us now, Deuce. We wearing state whites? We cuffed and chained? Hell, no. Last time I looked, this was a brand-new big-bucks car you and me is riding in."

"Give you that, Mertts. We walked out, we dint waste no time."

"We put the cluck back in the chicken pronto."

"When they turnt us loose . . ." Teddy paused, thinking about the feeling of walking past those prison gates. "When they turnt us loose, was several matters I hadda take care of right away. One, a good haircut. Two, new suita clothes. Tree, some decent action wit cash flow."

"Well, we ain't done too bad for a couple boys three, four weeks outta the Texas Department of Corrections." Mertts pointed straight ahead, toward downtown. "See the way that fog looks kinda smeared over all them lights? Know what it reminds me of? Vicks VapoRub. Come in a blue jar and your mama'd put it on your chest when you had a cold."

His mama. Violet Mertts, a large, gray-haired woman who liked to bet the dogs, had picked them up when they got out of prison. Teddy and Mertts spent three days with her, in her tiny house that smelled of mildew. It was an hour out of Houston, somewhere in the sticks, making Teddy wish one more time that he'd never left New York.

She called Mertts her Little Dancing Bear. Telling Teddy, my Little Dancing Bear was never like this before, never had a fight in his life, was just the sweetest boy until the accident. Teddy said, "You mean the golf club in his head? That accident?" "It changed everything," she said, showing Teddy a sad face, while in the next room Mertts popped more pills.

Violet Mertts just about drove Teddy nuts yakking all the time. But the really strange thing about her: she actually kept money in the cookie jar. Teddy thought people only did that on TV. She had close to 125 bucks in there, her dog track winnings, which Teddy stashed in his pocket one night while she was taking a bath.

Now Duff's Jag made a half-orbit of downtown Dallas and headed up North Central. As they neared the Haskell exit Mertts said, "You're looking kinda tense, Deuce. You think you been getting enough sleep?"

"Sleep don't got nothing to do widdit. I got business here to take care of." Teddy took a deep breath and tried to relax himself. Just thinking about it made his insides burn. "The reason I got sent down to Huntsville inna first place? Motherfucker in Dallas dimed me. Made the phone call to the cops personally, Mertts. Dialed 'em up wit his own finger."

"Well, shit, whyn't you say so long time ago? All you had to say was, Fredrick, lessgo to Big D and fuck up a rat. I woulda said, Point the way. That's what I woulda told you."

Teddy looked at him, then shook his head. Thinking, This guy, man . . . "That's what you said already, Mertts. When we left Houston, you said, Point the way."

Mertts beamed and gave two thumbs up. "My point exactly, Deuce."

They stole a couple of flashlights at a Stop N Go, Teddy nabbing them while Mertts paid for a carton of orange juice. After that, Teddy had to wander around East Dallas a bit—it had been three years since his arrest—but he finally found what he was looking for: an old garage apartment, well off the street. "This is where the motherfucker lives," Teddy said. The apartment was dark, with no car in front.

Mertts peered across the unlit weedy yard. "Looks like ain't nobody home."

Teddy parked at the curb and picked up his flashlight as he opened the car door. "You coming or not?"

At the front step of the apartment they walked over some old newspapers and a new phone book that was sealed in clear shrinkwrap. Two kicks from Mertts and the apartment door splintered open. Mertts said, "After you, Deuce." Teddy followed his bouncing flashlight beam up the stairs. Calling as he went, "Yoo-hoo, asshole, I'm back."

But at the top Teddy found only empty rooms—abandoned trash scattered on the floor, the stale air holding a slight smell of old garbage and decayed wood. For years he had been thinking about what he would do at this moment, and now there was no one to do it with.

By the time Teddy made it back downstairs, Mertts was sitting on the first step with the phone book open in his lap. "Maybe this'll tell us where he went." Mertts shined his flashlight on the pages. "What's the rat's name, anyway?"

Teddy glanced back upstairs, remembering what had happened there. Remembering the way he had been locked to the sink drainpipe up in the bathroom, chained like a dog, left there so long he'd pissed his pants.

His insides fired up again. Teddy turned from the doorway and told Mertts, "See if that fucking phone book has a Jack Flippo in it."

They went back to the Stop N Go, where Teddy shoplifted a map. He used it to find the street listed in the directory next to Jack Flippo's name. It was up in the suburbs past LBJ, a half-hour drive.

"Boy's come up in the world," Mertts said as they parked at

the curb in front of a brick home. The only light burning was one above the front door. "Check that little sign stuck in the flower bed? Dude's got hisself an alarm system, Deuce."

Teddy opened the car door. "Asshole's gonna need more than an alarm."

Mertts grabbed his sleeve. "Hold on, now. What are you gonna do?"

Teddy knocked Mertts's hand off. "Don't wrinkle the jacket."

"Gotta think this through, Deuce. I mean, what's your plan? Go kick the door in, like last time?"

"Kick the door, then kick ass."

"And listen to the alarm si-reen go off? Deuce, you're one of the smartest boys I ever met, but I been breaking into houses since I was ten years old. How about listening to the pro on this one?"

"You got a idea or you just jerking off at the mout?"

"'Course I got an idea. First thing you do is steer us around back."

Teddy drove to the alley, an empty path for the garbage trucks between backyard fences. A few street lamps gave the fog a dim orange-pink glow. Some dogs barked, but blocks away.

"Hang loose, Deuce, I'll be right back." Mertts got out of the car, climbed a six-foot wooden fence, and jumped into the back yard.

Five minutes later the garage door opened. Mertts walked out with a smile. "Ain't nobody home. But there's a doormat that says 'Welcome' on it. I think that means us."

Inside, they leaned against the kitchen counter, having a couple of Heinekens from the refrigerator. "I seen he didn't have the windows wired up," Mertts said. "Most people don't, 'cause that's where you run into the real cost. Know what I'm saying, Deuce?"

"Yeah, whatever." Teddy looked around at all the appliances and kitchenware, at the copper pots hanging from a rack over the stove. This fucking Jack Flippo had changed.

"So I pop one of the back windows and shimmy in," Mertts said. "I got my eyes peeled for a infrared and don't see a damn thing."

Teddy studied the breadmaker on the kitchen counter and wondered how much he could get for something like that at a pawnshop.

"So I get myself to this door here." Mertts shot a thumb over his shoulder. "I'm looking for a keypad for the alarm system, right? Some people make it easy for you and write the code number on the wall right next to the keypad. They do, I shit you not, Deuce."

What amazed Teddy was how clean the kitchen looked. He could put his silk jacket down anywhere and not have to worry.

"But there ain't no keypad." Mertts pointed again to the door. "The sumbitch has got a sign out front, but he don't have no system. Just thought he'd outsmart everbody."

Teddy turned toward Mertts. "Yeah, a smartass. You got that right."

The two of them walked into the living room, and Teddy had a hard time believing his eyes when he found the light switch: two leather couches and a big-screen TV.

"I think we chill here," Teddy said, "and wait for the motherfucker to show."

Teddy looked for something to watch while Mertts moved the car halfway down the block. They had a few more beers and relaxed on the couches, taking in two episodes of *Baywatch* and an infomercial about making a million in real estate with no money down. "Guy's talking some sense, you know it?" Teddy said.

Around eleven they heard the garage door going up. Teddy killed the TV and the lamp. The door to the kitchen opened and shut. There was the sound of footsteps in the darkened kitchen, then down the hall to the back of the house. Next they heard running water. After a couple of minutes Mertts said, "Deuce, I think the dude's taking a shower."

"He's gonna die clean, then."

"Lemme grab him for you." Mertts got up and went toward the back of the house. Teddy sat in the dark. Imagining, like a kid thinking about dessert, what he was going to do to Jack Flippo.

There were some shouts and a few knocks against the wall. A minute later they were coming up the hallway, with Mertts saying, "Keep going, that's right."

The lights went on. Teddy smiled and said, "Hey, asshole, remem—" He stopped.

Mertts said, "Well?" He was holding a leather belt tightened around the neck of a wet, scared, naked man. "Well?" Mertts said again.

"It ain't him," Teddy said.

Mertts bent over and looked at the man's face. "You sure, Deuce?"

"Fuck, yes, I'm sure. It's the wrong guy." Teddy got up and stood in front of the naked man. "Where's Jack Flippo? Loosen him up, Mertts, so he can talk." Teddy waited, letting the man cough a little and get his breath. Then, "Jack Flippo? When's he coming home?"

The man shook his head as much as he could. Mertts tightened the belt. The man's eyes bugged out and he went up on his toes. "You wanna be a hard case?" Teddy said. "Be some kinda shitbird and protect your buddy Jack?"

Teddy was about to give the guy a backhand across the face, but he didn't have his rubber gloves on. You started worrying about hygiene, he thought, and torture got complicated. Teddy said, "Loosen him up, Mertts, he's tryna tell me something."

When the belt slackened the man coughed and gasped, then said, "There's no Jack here."

Teddy looked left and right. "Think I hant seen that already?"

The man was trembling but he was getting his voice back. "I don't know who you're talking about."

With his free hand Mertts pulled the folded phone book page from his pocket. "What's it say right here, mister?" He held the page in front of the man's face. "Go ahead, take it. Take the paper, goddamnit."

Shaky hands came up to grasp the paper. "Now," Mertts said. "Look under . . . hey, Deuce, what's the rat's name again?"

"I'm asking one last time," Teddy said. "Where's Jack Flippo?"

"Look at that page," Mertts said, "and tell us you don't know who we're talking about. If I was you, I'd start spilling."

The man stared at the paper. "This says—" He was blinking, with tears rolling down his cheeks. "This says the man you want lives on Vickery."

"Fuckin-A right," Teddy said.

"But this is Vickers. You've got—" The man sobbed. "You've got the wrong street."

Teddy and Mertts stared at each other. The man broke free and ran to the far end of the room. With nowhere else to go, he did something Teddy had never seen before: He tried to climb the wall.

"I had that feeling a few times," Teddy said as Mertts moved toward the man. "It's where you ain't got nothing in your corner but the corner."

# 7

$\mathcal{J}$ack was up early, driving in the fog before sunrise, ready to give Sherri Plunkett a full day's work. Thinking as he drove: A sad fact, but a lot of his clients were suckers.

People hired detectives because they were suspicious, but most of them hoped their suspicions were wrong. The husband says he's working late but comes home smelling of Chanel No. 5? The sucker says maybe there's an innocent reason. Or there's a 100-grand hole in the company books and the partner was last seen boarding a flight to Mexico? Perhaps, the sucker says, it could all be explained.

They all wanted happy endings. Jack hadn't found one yet.

Which led him to sad fact number two: The more money you had, the greater the chance that someone was trying to get his hands on it. And Sherri Plunkett had buckets of money.

He parked in a nearly empty lot and walked upstairs to his office in the Greenie's Building, atop Greenie's 24 HR Coffee Shop on East Grand Avenue. Jack had one room with a couch, a metal desk, a two-line phone, a computer, and a printer.

The smell of frying bacon floated up from downstairs. Jack spun his Rolodex, looking for the number of Miles Wesley, a private investigator he had used before to run the traps for him in Los Angeles. He found the number and dialed. An answering machine picked up—what Jack had expected, given the hour.

48

On his machine, Miles Wesley came across like a sitcom hipster. Saying, "Yo, what it is," and "Drop a message on me." Jack rolled his eyes and told Miles Wesley's tape what he wanted: Find out what he could about Sandra Danielle. And check out the two people who adopted her. The mother's dead, Jack said, but see if the father will talk.

He laid a few more details on Miles, then started a file on the Sherri Plunkett case. Jack typed what he knew into the computer and printed it, filling a couple of sheets.

After coffee and the newspaper at Greenie's, just past eight, he called a friend at Parkland. Joe Alexander, who used to be a legman with the DA, now was chief of security at the hospital. Big fat Joe, who wore purple polyester shirts and was always sweating, no matter how cold outside or how smooth in the office. Everything was a crisis with Joe.

"I need a birth record from nineteen sixty-two," Jack told him. He spelled Sherri Plunkett's maiden name. "I'm looking for the daddy."

"Oh, Lord, that could take a week," Joe moaned. "Those records, jeez, who knows . . ." But not long after noon Joe called back. Jack had a club sandwich from Greenie's half finished when he picked up the phone. "You found it already?" Jack said. "Hey, you move fast for an old man."

Joe didn't laugh. He said, "Christ, Jack, tell me you're not chasing this asshole again."

"What are you talking about?"

"You saying you don't know?"

"Don't know what? All I want is the father's name."

"Whatever you say, buddy. I mean, if you have to have it, I got the record right here in front of me. Right here on my desk, staring back at me. Oh, boy. I would ask you if your pencil's ready, but I got a feeling you won't need one, because this one you won't forget."

Jack idly brushed some dust from his boot as he listened to

49

Joe's buildup. He could imagine Joe as a doctor. Telling a patient with a cold: Sure, you'll recover from this. But just remember, sooner or later everyone has to die.

"Don't think I can put this off any longer," Joe said. He sighed once, then did it again. "Father's name, Jack, was Norton Lamar Luttrall."

Jack thanked Joe, hung up the phone, and pushed his sandwich away. For once, Joe had been right to lay on the grief.

Putting Norton Luttrall in prison was going to save Vanessa Ingram's career. Jack was supposed to help.

Norton Luttrall was an ex–bail bondsman who was rumored to have killed at least two people. Torchin' Norton was the best unconvicted arsonist in Dallas. The fire department, the DA, and the insurance companies chased him for years and never made a case. The buildings kept burning down, but Norton still walked the streets.

This time, though, they had a witness.

The blaze at Creekside Village Gardens was instant four alarms one predawn. It also was prime arson turf: an unfinished apartment complex whose developer walked the edge of bust. Nobody knew about the transient who had been sleeping in one of the units until firemen found his body.

Not long after that Dallas police caught Darden Ellis trying to hot-wire a car from a sales lot. Darden was a skinny, jumpy little headache of a man with a long sheet of priors. He stuttered. Everybody called him Duh-duh-Darden. When he was popped for the car theft, he started talking. Saying, "D-d-drop the charges and I'll make Norton Luttrall g-good for the C-c-creekside Village arson." They did, he did, and Assistant District Attorney Vanessa Ingram got the case.

Vanessa Ingram's dark hair showed a few streaks of gray, though she still pulled her share of attention in the courthouse corridors, still caught hungry stares from the fat bailiffs. But she didn't carry herself the way she once did, back when she looked like someone zooming to the top of the DA's office. By the time Jack met her there were whispers around the place that her drinking had tanked her career.

With a few high-profile losses and an appeals court reversal for prosecutorial misconduct, Vanessa was almost out the door. District Attorney Johnny Hector never said it officially, but he made it clear to Vanessa that nailing Norton Luttrall was the only way she'd keep her job.

She was forty-three and three times divorced. Vanessa wore her sadness everywhere, put it on every morning before she got out of bed. Jack knew this because some mornings he was there beside her.

He was new to the DA's staff then, in his twenties and not yet married. Vanessa needed someone to work second chair on the Norton Luttrall case. She also needed someone to have drinks with and someone to take her home at night.

They seemed to be a good team. Jack was green but knew how to line up witnesses and assemble information so a jury could follow it all. He knew to sit and listen when it was late and Vanessa Ingram had put away too much and she started crying, talking about how bad she wanted this piece of crap Norton Luttrall, how this case was going to pull her out of the pit she'd been falling into if Duh-duh-Darden didn't fuh-fuh-fuck up on the stand.

Darden Ellis, as it turned out, was nowhere near Creekside Village Gardens the night they burned. Darden Ellis wasn't even in the same state.

Vanessa Ingram didn't show up in court that last day. She walked out of the DA's office and never came back. Jack was the one who had to stand before the judge, swallow hard, and move for a dismissal of all charges against Norton Luttrall.

He had tried not to think about Vanessa Ingram much since then, except for a few times late at night, after a couple of drinks, when he was in the mood to torture himself.

\*      \*      \*

Jack walked downstairs to Greenie's for another cup of coffee. Thinking, Norton-goddamn-Luttrall. Saying it out loud a couple of times and shaking his head. Jack remembered how Norton had looked in the courtroom: a stooped man, getting old, with a face like a buzzard whose business was slow.

The last anybody'd heard of him, as far as Jack knew, Norton had gone to Florida. Announced to his lawyer that he was goddamn tired of getting hassled all over Dallas for bullshit he hadn't done, and he was sixty-what years old, so it was time to go sit on a beach.

Chances were good he was dead by now. Ten years ago he looked as if he could go any day, and Jack would bet that day had come. But Jack went back upstairs and put his fingers to his computer keyboard anyway. He called up a database used by skip tracers—a file of names and addresses taken from phone company records, utility connections, tax rolls, and magazine subscription lists. He wasn't sure why he bothered, but what could it hurt? He typed in Norton's name.

It didn't take a minute to get an answer. Jack stared at the letters on the screen, blinked twice, and stared again. Norton Lamar Luttrall, it said. Current address, 403 Jasper Avenue, Dallas, Texas.

He looked out the window, up East Grand. Maybe he couldn't spot Jasper Avenue from his perch, but he could walk there in fifteen minutes. Torchin' Norton was practically his neighbor.

Jack thought again about that last day in court ten years ago. When Norton heard the judge's dismissal he beamed, hugged his lawyer, stuck an unlit cigar in his mouth, and started his shuffle to the exit. He had to pass the prosecution table on the way. Jack, putting files into his briefcase, looked up to see Norton extending a hand to shake.

Jack let the hand hang there long enough that most men would have pulled it away. Norton kept it out, a little unsteady maybe, but staying there for Jack to grab it. Finally Jack reached and gave an obligatory one-pump.

Norton took his cigar out of his mouth and pointed the wet end at Jack. "Give you some advice?" Norton said. "You're in the wrong line of work, bub."

The words came back to Jack as he pulled his car to the curb in front of 403 Jasper. It was a neat clapboard house in a neighborhood that was trying hard not to fall apart. The porch had a swing and some flowers in pots.

A Mexican woman wearing a white apron answered the bell. "Mr. Luttrall in?" Jack said. She opened the door without a word. Jack stepped inside and followed voices through the kitchen to a sunporch at the back of the house. Two old men sat at a card table in a blue cloud of cigar smoke. One, wearing a yachting cap, was in a wheelchair. The other, Norton, rested on a metal folding chair. Both of them moved dominoes around on the table with dry, bony hands. Jack looked at Norton and said, "Do you remember me?"

Norton didn't glance up. "I'm seventy-two years old, and I don't remember a damn thing before yesterday. Were you here yesterday?"

"No."

"Then I don't remember you."

"We met about ten—"

"But I'll take a guess." Norton pulled his eyes from the dominoes and looked him over. "I'll guess you're here to sell me a cemetery plot. What do you think, Commander? Think he's one of the funeral-home boys?"

The man in the wheelchair gave Jack a watery-eyed study and nodded. "You might be right."

"Goddamn right I'm right." Norton picked up his cigar. "It's a deal, bub, I'll buy a grave from you." Two puffs on the cigar. "But only if you jump in first and pull the dirt in after you."

Jack moved a third chair to the table and sat. "Not selling any cemetery plots, Norton."

"Strangers who come to your house and smile, they're always selling something. Right, Commander?"

"Maybe."

"No damn maybe about it."

Norton was thin and bent, and his wisps of white hair looked as if they were tired of growing. But his voice was strong and his dark eyes clear. Jack said, "The last time you and I spoke—"

"Uh-oh, Commander, she found you." Norton looked past Jack's shoulder. Jack turned to see a large woman in a nurse's uniform. "It's the enema patrol and she's tracked you down." Norton pointed his cigar at the nurse. "Next time we'll lock the door."

"Let's go, Mr. C." The nurse took the handgrips of the wheelchair and began to push the chair toward the front door.

"Tell her not to starve you," Norton said as they went. "You look like a skeleton with skin hanging on it. Hey, nursie, give the man some food."

When they had gone Norton turned to Jack. "My next-door neighbor. I told him, hire somebody that can work the kitchen. I mean, forget the nurse and get a cook." He pointed the cigar Jack's way. "Your honest opinion. You think that's the way to go, hire a cook?"

"That might make sense."

"Goddamn right it makes sense."

Jack said, "As I was saying, the last—"

"What time you got?"

Jack checked his watch. "Five after one."

"Shit." Norton rose from the chair, joints cracking. "I tell her every day, fix me a cup of coffee when it's one o'clock. Does she do it? Hell, no. Here's my advice, bub. Don't hire a maid that can't understand the American native tongue."

Norton brushed by him and into the house. Jack followed as he went to a couch in the living room. Norton yelled, "Juana?

Coffee!" Then he lit a cigar. "Macanudo," he said. "Best damn cigar outside Havana, you know it?"

Jack nodded. "Whatever you say."

"Now you're talking."

Jack looked around the room. It was tidy enough, but there wasn't much to see. Maybe a dozen books and a couple of empty brass candlestick holders taking up a shelf. On the wall, some framed prints of generic mountain landscapes behind dusty glass. On the coffee table, a few copies of *Reader's Digest* and *National Geographic.*

"You see this?" Norton opened one of the *Geographics* where he had turned down the corner of one page. "This is something else. Country over in Africa, you get a special hand-carved coffin, custom-designed just for you. Based on what you did with your life, see." He put a long, thin finger on the page. "Look here. Fisherman gets buried in a big fish. Guy who likes dogs gets planted in a big dog. Coal-truck driver gets a coal truck, with mirrors and a taillight." Norton puffed and watched the smoke. "Think I'd make mine a big Macanudo. How about you?"

Jack's mind had wandered off to visit Vanessa Ingram again. He shook his head and said, "I'm sorry—what?"

"Your coffin. What kind, bub?"

Jack cleared his throat. "Haven't given it much thought."

"You think you're gonna live to be an old man like me. Well, think about this: Could be your number's up next week. Could be tomorrow. You don't know. Do you?"

"You're probably right."

"No probably about it. Turn your head for ten seconds, the whole world can change while you're not looking." Norton removed his cigar, like unplugging a hole, and shouted, "Juana!"

The woman appeared. "Could we please have our coffee now?" Norton said. She nodded and went back to the kitchen. Norton shook his head. "No telling what we'll get." He looked at

Jack. "Well, you didn't come here to talk about coffins. What was it you wanted?"

"You remember me?"

"I remember."

"I was one of the assistant DAs on your case ten years—"

"I just said I remember. Christ, we got two people in this house now that don't speak English?"

Juana brought two cups of coffee on a plastic tray. "Thank you, very nice," Norton said. "Now, could you bring me some cream? Cream. For the coffee." He made a pouring motion over the cup. "*El creamo.*"

Juana nodded and left. Norton looked Jack over. "You know why I went to Florida?"

Jack reached for a cup. "To get away would be my guess."

"No damn guessing about it. I had to leave Dallas, 'cause if I didn't I woulda killed that little worm. You know who I'm talking about?"

"Sure."

"I'm talking about that scrawny fart in a jar you and your friends dredged up to testify against me."

"Darden was worried about payback."

"Worried ain't the word he shoulda been."

Juana brought a small carton of milk. Norton filled his cup to the brim and stirred fast while his cigar smoldered in an ashtray. "That lying little cocksucker, he thought he'd save his butt and take Norton Luttrall down at the same time. Tell you something, bub. Ten years ago? I'm walking down the street and I seen that stuttering piece of sewage? It woulda taken five wrestlers and a sailor to pry my fingers off his throat." Still stirring, the spoon pinging against the inside of the cup, but not spilling a drop. "That's why I hadda go to Florida. To cool down."

Jack could see the throbbing blue veins in the papery skin of Norton's temple. The old man breathed hard through a beaked nose. Saying, "I shoulda cut him up and fed him to the goats." He waved a hand. "All right, that motor's ran outta gas. He walked in here today I'd probably give him something to drink. Just like I'm doing for you. You, the guy that wanted to put me in prison."

"I'm long gone from the DA. It's all private work for me now."

"I shoulda sued the bunch of you. False prosecution, I coulda made a million. I could be on a yacht in the Gulf of Mexico now instead of passing gas around here."

"Maybe so." Jack watched Norton lift the cup halfway, drop his mouth to it, and slurp. "When we're through walking memory lane here I want to ask you about something else."

Norton ran his dark eyes over Jack, then raised a finger and pointed. "The second I seen you walk in the door this morning? Know what I said to myself?"

Jack shook his head.

"I said, here's today's pain in the ass."

"I just have a few questions on a client's behalf."

"All those years, there musta been a rule down at the police department: If you can't solve a crime, just arrest Norton Luttrall. You don't believe me, do you."

"I believe you."

"All right, I'll give you an example. Nineteen sixty-two, somebody blew up Chicken Harris at a dice house in West Dallas. Somebody did the world a favor and put a bomb under his car. You remember that?"

"I was still in diapers in nineteen sixty-two," Jack said.

"Pieces of Chicken was still falling from the sky when the plainclothes banged on my door with a warrant. Remember what happened?"

"I'll guess that you got off."

"Ain't no need to guess, bub, I'll tell you exactly what happened. I got no-billed."

Jack held up a hand like a cop stopping traffic. "What I wanted to ask you about—"

"Nineteen sixty-five, Joe Gentile's house goes up in flames with him in it. Remember him?"

"That was before—"

"Worst cocksucker that ever laced up a pair of shoes, Joe Gentile. People of Dallas should have thrown a party for whoever smoked him. Shoulda named a street after the man that had the guts to take care of Joe Gentile. Well, you can guess what happened. Two minutes after the fire's out, the cops bring Norton Luttrall downtown. Norton Luttrall, who don't have a single solitary felony conviction, but they got me downtown in a little room and want me to tell 'em I'm the one that took Joe Gentile off the books. Even though they don't got enough evidence to feed two flies." Norton shook his head in disgust. "That case didn't go nowhere but the garbage, bub."

When Norton finally paused, Jack jumped in. "You recall Sherri Plunkett? Sherri LeBonne when you knew her."

Norton picked up his cigar, now dead, from the ashtray. He lit a wooden match with his thumbnail. "Danced at Louie Chick's place on Commerce when I knew her. Cute little girl. Wiggled better than most, seems to me."

"Have you seen her lately?"

Norton puffed and dropped the match in the ashtray. "Not since the Dead Sea was just sick. You got any real questions, bub?"

Jack reached into the pocket of his shirt and pulled out a piece of paper folded in quarters. "When's the last time you saw your daughter?"

Norton smoked and seemed to focus on the far wall. After a while he said, barely loud enough for Jack to hear, "I don't have a daughter."

Jack opened the paper and glanced at what he had written. "Born at Parkland Hospital, child of Sherri with an *i* LeBonne and Norton Lamar Luttrall." Norton's stare stayed on the wall.

"The reason I ask," Jack said, "is that your daughter, Sandra, came to live with her mother not too long ago. After her adoptive mom died, she tracked Sherri down. She came from Los Angeles to see Sherri and has been living with her since."

Norton rolled his gaze slowly Jack's way. The air seemed to go out of him. "You're not making any sense," he said, almost a whisper.

"The reason I'm here, the reason I'm asking you questions—" Jack watched Norton's face go hard as he pulled away somewhere, like a crab sloughing its shell. "A few weeks ago," Jack said, "someone started stalking Sandra. Even tried to grab her one night. I'm wondering if you have any idea what's going on. Has she contacted you? Said anything to you about it?"

Norton stood without looking at Jack and walked slowly toward the back of the house. "We're through talking," he said as he left the room.

**D**ean Dudley couldn't believe all the work that went into a kidnapping: First, purchase materials. Next, find a place to stash everything. After that, do your basic design on where to make the grab and how to demand the drop. Then, figure out where to run to once you got the money. All this thinking made him tired. Snatching somebody was as hard as having a real job. Dean had to guess about that last part.

He spent a few minutes in the Texas-shaped pool to refresh himself. But the troubles and worries wouldn't stop swooping and diving, like big birds pecking at Dean's head. What if the police somehow found out? What if the car broke down during the snatch? What if Captain Flying Dickhead got too close again?

From the beginning this deal was just supposed to be a quick pick for cash, and now it had turned into some kind of production. And all of it to get what should have been his in the first place. All of it because of *her*.

Dean stared at Sherri's upstairs bedroom window and worked himself to a boil. Thinking, The biggest bitch in six states and I'm married to her. Telling himself, You're the man, you're the husband. No reason in the world you shouldn't have half her money. Why the hell else get married? He stepped from the water, wrapped a towel around his waist, and made straight for the house. Time to straighten this out.

He took the stairs two at a time and blew into Sherri's bedroom without knocking. It was just after three in the afternoon.
He knew exactly where she'd be at this hour—in bed, wearing
her black sleeping mask, like Zorro without the eyeholes. He'd
wake her old-lady ass up and do business.

But the bed was empty. She'd be in the tub, then, taking her
daily two-hour bubble bath and doing her nails. Dean threw
open the door to the bathroom. Nothing there. He stalked back
into the bedroom. The woman slept from two to four every afternoon. Every afternoon, except the one when Dean needed her to
be here so he could tell her what's what.

It always happened this way, and Dean couldn't understand.
If Dean tried to step over the line, do something different, someone always wanted to chop his toes off. Always. But other people—they did what they wanted. They came and went, and
nobody asked them where they were going or where they had
been. They got the easy money and had a good time, and they
didn't have to explain dick about it. Other people, they—

"You're dripping water on the carpet," Sherri said. Dean
whirled toward the voice. Sherri sat in a velvet-covered chair in
the far corner. She said, "That's why there's a cabana by the pool,
Dean. So people can put on dry clothes before they come in the
house."

Dean squared to face her. "You and me have some important
things to talk about."

"That'll be the day."

"Listen to me. I need ten thousand dollars cash money right
now. And I don't have time to argue about it. It's for business,
that's everything you need to know."

"Here's everything *you* need to know, hon. Forget it."

It was all Dean could do to keep from ramming his fist into
her face. Just one sweet punch across the mouth. He almost melted, thinking how good it would feel. Dean closed his eyes for a
couple of seconds. Then, "It's a business transaction, okay? And

it's gotta be done this week. So I need the money, like, now."

Sherri brushed some lint off the front of her midnight blue silk pajamas. "How long've we been married, Dean? Three months? Four?"

Long enough, Dean thought, to see I made a big mistake. He said, "Doesn't really matter how long, does it? 'Cause we are man and wife last time I looked, which means certain things get shared, seems to me. Bank accounts being one of 'em. I ain't kidding, Sherri. I gotta have this money before I leave the house today."

That got a long, slow blink from her. Dean said, "Sherri, don't screw with me now. Don't give me a hard time about this. 'Cause there's things at work here you don't understand. I can't say nothing else about it. Just listen to me when I say things could happen that you don't know nothing about. Things you wouldn't like."

She raised a painted eyebrow. "You think so?"

"Sherri, there's shit going on that would knock your socks off if you was wearing any. But the beauty of it, see, is that I can handle it. Dean Dudley'll make it all go away, and you won't ever know there was a problem. All you have to do is understand that you and me are married, and that means we're supposed to share everything. You can start by cutting me ten thousand today. Matter of fact, better make it twenty."

Sherri gave a little laugh. "Your brain must be like the fuse box in an old house, Dean. You get the toaster and hair dryer and the washing machine going all at once, and the circuits just blow."

"Don't try to confuse me now, Sherri. I gotta have—"

"Why don't you just do what you did last time? Why don't you go ahead and steal some of my checks? Do that and forge the signature, just like last time. Well?"

Dean hadn't been ready for that one. He tried to answer and nothing came out.

"You didn't think I knew about that little trick, did you?" Sherri stood. "Something you might not have snapped to, Dean? Every month the bank sends me all the checks drawn on my account. Think I don't know which ones I wrote? Think I don't know my own signature?"

"Hey, that wasn't stealing."

"Three checks, five thousand each."

"See, this is what I'm trying to tell you. It's my money, too. When that preacher said, 'to have and to hold,' that's what he was talking about."

Sherri looked at the floor, talking to herself. "Lesson number one," she said. "Don't ever get married just because you find yourself drunk and horny."

"Besides," Dean said, "that bank's no damn good anyway. Last time I was there they tried to tell me the account was closed."

"Hell yes, it was closed. I closed it, soon as I found out you were robbing me blind."

"And you didn't tell your own husband? You know how humiliating it was, Sherri, trying to cash one of those checks and have some dude in a suit kissing me off?"

Sherri brought her eyes back to him and shook her head. "You re something else. I don't know what, exactly, but something."

Dean could feel the pressure building, as if someone had ıck a hose in his chest and pumped in too much heat. Telling nself: Stay calm, now, and lay it out for her, give her one more nce. He held up one hand as if taking an oath. "All right, rri, I'll shoot it to you straight ahead, no bullshit. I bet on : games, all right?"

Sherri laughed. "You did what?"

I know what I'm doing, all right? I've been at this a long It's just that I got in a little deeper lately. You understand?"

Io answer from Sherri as she put her jeweled lighter to a ·tte.

Dean said, "I was all set to get it back, okay? Every bit. If one shot doesn't fall, just one shot, I win everything back and I'm a free man." He shrugged and ducked his head. "What can I tell you? It didn't happen that way. . . . So I need the money like right now."

She waited a few seconds before saying, "No chance."

Dean's voice came out high and loud. "You know what those motherfuckers do if you don't pay? Do you?"

Sherri stood, took a long draw, and blew the smoke out slowly. The bitch had all the time in the world. "No, Dean, I don't."

"You wanna know what they do? I'll tell you what they do. They start breaking bones. One finger a day for every day you're late. When they run out of fingers, they move on to your arms and legs."

Sherri thought it over, then said, "That's bad news."

"It sure as shit is."

"'Cause I was hoping they'd just kill you right away."

Dean heard a roar inside as he stepped forward and pushed Sherri against the wall. The air came out of her in a small burst. Dean balled his fist, ready to pound it right into her mouth.

But he stopped, his fist in the air. Thinking, what if he hit her and she called the police? He gets arrested, and his big scheme, his chance for a big payday, goes up in smoke.

Dean backed away. Saying "You'll be fucking sorry" as he turned and walked from the room. At the door Dean glanced back at her, and the sight broke his stride.

She had a smile on her face.

# 9

"I can't believe I dint take off my jacket. Lookadis snag." Teddy Tunstra II pointed to a couple of errant threads on his sleeve. "One hundred percent pure silk, totally ruint now, all because we hadda haul some guy up into his attic."

Teddy drove east on Mockingbird Lane. Late afternoon, sunny and warm. Mertts watched the scenery from the Jaguar's passenger seat. "What choice we got?" Mertts said. "Leave him in his own living room? Solid dead and butt naked, with a belt around his neck? That, Deuce, might arouse some suspicion."

"I got one word to say to you, Mertts." Teddy jerked a thumb to the back. "The trunk udda car. The motherfucker's car was right there, we shoulda used it. Hey, in New York? Half the bodies that get stashed, get stashed inna trunk. Maybe tree quarters of 'em, you don't count the ones get tossed inna river."

Mertts shook his head. "Somebody's missing, people searching for him head straight to the nearest trunk, I shit you not. Say this dude don't show at Aunt Tillie's house tonight for supper like he's supposed to. Aunt Tillie sends cousin Elmo over to see what's happened to him. House is empty but the car's there, here's the first place cousin Elmo looks?"

"His name's Elmo? Then he's too fucking dumb to look anywhere."

"He looks in the trunk, that's where. Elmo pops the lid and 's the whole kitten kaboodle right there."

65

Teddy glanced at a street sign. "I think I shoulda turned couple blocks back."

"Besides, Deuce, it's just a coat."

"The fuck you saying, Mertts? It's a one hundred percent silk
jacket." Teddy stopped for a red light, then brushed at the snag
on his sleeve. "You talk like silk grows on trees."

Mertts studied the map in his lap. "I believe we turn right at
the next street. Pretty sure. These things are damn hard to read."

"The other thing I'm pissed about?" Teddy burned rubber off
the light, then made the turn. "We wasted the whole day wit you
inna sack back there. We coulda been rolling, and you're sleeping instead."

Mertts rubbed the L-shaped scar. "Deuce, I get these pains,
man. C'mon, you know that. Ain't nothing to do but pop some
Talwins and curl up in bed. Six or seven hours later, maybe nine
or ten if it's a bad one, I'm pretty fresh. Hey, you gotta stay fresh."

"No, you gotta *look* fresh. Big difference. Which is why
Teddy Deuce shunt be hauling dead prickolas up some shitty little stairs."

Mertts checked the map again. "Next left, and that oughta
do it."

They turned down a street flanked by small older houses,
most of them well tended but nothing fancy. Teddy checked the
number from the phone book page and stopped in front of a gray
bungalow whose lawn needed trimming.

As they walked across the yard Mertts said, "We got the right
house this time? This busting into the wrong one is like getting
your mouth all set for a steak dinner and they give you Vienna
sausage."

Teddy mounted the porch and knocked hard five times on
the front door. "He ain't here this time? I'm gonna be plenty
pissed off, believe that."

"Or," Mertts said, "you ever had a dream where you're just
about to do this babe, but something wakes you up before you
can slide and glide?"

Teddy knocked some more. "We're talking off-the-scale pissed off here."

"And just try getting back to sleep with the idea you're gonna have the same dream with the same babe. Don't work that way. A dream ain't a damn comic book, Deuce. You don't put it down and pick it up."

Teddy studied the front door and windows. "You see an alarm?"

Mertts stepped from the porch and walked to the side of the house. "Not with these baby blues."

"How about neighbors?"

"Don't spot a soul."

"Then do your stuff."

Mertts crouched before the front door. Twenty seconds and they were in the house.

Teddy went straight for the bedrooms, thinking how sweet it would be to cruise in with the chump snoozing. Say, how's this for a good morning? But he discovered an unmade bed with no one in it. The other rooms were empty, too.

Mertts was going through a stack of mail in the kitchen when Teddy walked in. "This time I checked," Mertts said, holding up an unopened electric bill. "We finally got the right guy. Says it here on the envelope, Jack Flippo."

"Just like that asshole to be gone when I show up. I'm tryna keep my cool"—Teddy slammed the refrigerator with the butt of his fist—"but this motherfucker won't let me."

"See what this says." Mertts reached for the answering machine on the counter and pressed the button next to the blinking red light. The tape rewound, the machine beeped, then a woman's voice said, "Hey, angel-for-hire, did we say five or five-thirty to meet at Wong Ho? Are you gone already? Oh, well, see you there. 'Bye."

Teddy checked his watch. "Fuckin-A, straight-up five right now."

"Wong Ho." Mertts rubbed his belly and smiled. "Feeling like some Chinese food myself, Deuce."

\*     \*     \*

"The last commercial I did was for Soft Rain shampoo." Sandra Danielle ran the fingers of both hands through her hair and put on a blissful smile. "Recognize that move?" She did it again. "We must have done fifty takes of that same shot. I mean, how many different ways can you stick your hands in your hair and act like it's better than sex? They kept saying, Give us more joy. I'm like, hey, it's only hair."

Jack ran his own fingers through his own hair, and found no joy. Swear to God it felt thinner than it had the day before.

"But," Sandra said, "it paid the rent. That, and a job I had for stomach medicine." She motioned the waiter over and pushed her bowl his way. "This soup's cold," she said. Then back to Jack, "Try chirping this line for six or seven hours: 'Honey, I won't let your diarrhea spoil our vacation.' The director was this jerk who used to do porno films, and he had the worst breath. Boy, that was the day I almost walked off the set."

"And give up show business?"

"Exactly." Sandra pointed her egg roll at Jack. "No matter how bad it got, it was still better than anything else."

Wong Ho, in a converted Dairy Queen on Bryan Street, was about half full with a mix of tradesmen, white collars, and couples. Cooks screamed Chinese at each other in the kitchen. Live eels and lobsters waited for the wok in two large glass tanks by the front door, a bubbling saltwater death row.

The waiter brought another bowl of egg drop soup. "This one very hot," he said.

Jack and Sandra sat at a table for four in the middle of the room. Sandra had perfect diction and straight white teeth.

She wore a black, backless minidress with bare legs and black three-inch heels with straps around the ankles. Even the busboys stopped and stared when she made her entrance. Now Jack looked at her and remembered how it felt to push your brake pedal to the floor while your car skidded across the ice, headed for a brick wall.

He said, "You say it was better than anything else, this life you had."

Sandra tried her soup and shook her head. "This is still cold."

"But you did leave it. You came here."

"Temporary." Sandra shoved the bowl aside and put more mustard on her egg roll. "Soon as my agent phones with something, I'll be back in L.A. That reminds me, I gotta call him this afternoon, see if I'm still reading next week for the all-girl remake of *Hogan's Heroes*." She flagged the waiter and said, "Could we try again on this soup? To get it, you know, really hot?"

Jack waited till her eyes came back to him. "Have you seen your real father yet?"

She screwed up her face. "My *what?*"

"You tracked your mom down. Why not your dad?"

"'Dad?' You mean the jerk who got Sherri pregnant? You mean the pump-and-run man?"

"He might still be around," Jack said. "He might be right here in Dallas."

"He might be at the next table. Who cares? Don't know who he is and don't want to know. Sherri's the one I wanted to see. That's all. I wanted to find my mother, not have a big family reunion."

"This lawyer you say you hired. How'd he find Sherri? Adoption records can be pretty tough to crack."

Sandra shrugged. "I paid him his fee, he got me what I wanted. We didn't talk technique."

They ate for half a minute without talking, two quiet people surrounded by the clatter and noise of the restaurant. Finally Jack said, "Something else I've been wondering about. With somebody chasing you, how come you're still hanging around like everything's fine and breezy?"

Sandra peeled the paper wrapping away from her chopsticks, took a bite of shrimp, and said, "This is pretty good, how's yours?"

"I'm thinking if I were you, with this kidnap attempt and all, I'd be under armed guard or out of town."

She smiled at him. "What I've noticed about you? You don't really talk, you just ask questions."

Jack gave up on his chopsticks and used a fork. "If somebody's after you, why don't you slip away to somewhere else?"

"Have I ever told you about the strangest job I ever had?" Sandra downed another shrimp and kept talking. "My first steady gig, seventeen years old, I'm stage assistant to Mr. Alexander Beauvois, best magician in San Diego, California. Know how some magicians pull rabbits out of their hats? Alexander Beauvois pulled snakes."

Jack waited, with the unanswered questions starting to stack up.

"I was in charge of the snakes." Sandra smiled again. "Creepy job, right? But here's what I learned: hold the snake real firm at the back of his head and he won't bite you. Doesn't matter what kind. Hold them in the right place and they can't hurt you. . . . Works with all kinds of snakes, even the ones with two legs."

Jack put his fork down. "One more time. Somebody's trying to kidnap you. Why are you still hanging around town?"

"You know what? Tell you a secret." Sandra stood and leaned across the table, her breasts against his arm. Jack could smell her hair and perfume. The hem of the dress was slipping up over the curve of her ass. Men at other tables stared. Sandra put her lips close to Jack's ear and whispered, "You worry too much."

Jack took a deep breath. He glanced toward the front window, and caught sight of two men getting out of a car. One of them he recognized.

"Listen to me," he said to Sandra. "Stand up right now and get out of here as fast as you can."

# 10

The last time Jack had seen Teddy Tunstra II was in court, when he watched from the spectators' seats as Teddy copped to manslaughter. Afterward, the assistant DA shook Jack's hand and said, "Thanks for helping us move this load of sewage off the streets." That was two years ago. Jack always figured Teddy would be back to see him, but maybe not in a Chinese restaurant in East Dallas.

Now Jack said to Sandra, "Get out. Go."

"Do what?"

He pushed her chair with his hand. "Something bad's about to happen. Get up and walk out now."

"You're joking, right?"

Teddy had opened the front door to Wong Ho and was six or seven steps into the dining room, moving their way with a big smile. He caught Jack's eye and called, "Yo, Jackie."

Jack kept his gaze on Teddy but said to Sandra, "Listen to me. Get out of here."

"What for?" She sounded puzzled in a happy way. "Hey, is that a friend of yours?"

Jack stood, ready to fight if he had to, checking to see if Teddy was wearing his latex gloves. Teddy reached the table with "How about this? Unfuckingbelievable. Jackie, bro, long time no see."

He was dressed in a full Teddy: expensive-looking jacket with a burgundy silk shirt open at the collar, thin gold chain catching light at his neck, taupe slacks with cuffs. No wrinkles anywhere. His braided loafers could have passed for slippers, and his hair was short and shiny with gel. The only thing not perfect was his nose. Its tip was a healed-over mangling that veered slightly left.

Teddy took one empty chair at the table. "Man, talk about weird. I just walk innis place and here you are. What are the odds of that, huh? How's it hanging for you, Jackie?"

In Teddy's wake, like a freighter after a speedboat, came the second man. He was five or six inches over six feet, and had the build of a pro wrestler who couldn't lay off the mashed potatoes and gravy. His eyes were heavy-lidded, his hair a nest of golden ringlets. He had a scar above one temple like a ragged zipper to his brain. The man wore a dark three-piece suit with no shirt. He took the fourth chair at the table and threw a nervous glance toward the bubbling tanks at the front.

"Tell you one damn thing," he said. "Them eels give me the creeps."

"Bet you dint expect to see me so fast," Teddy said. Jack stopped looking at the big man and turned toward Teddy's smile. "Bet you thought Teddy Deuce—hey, Jack, sit down, let's talk— bet you thought Teddy Deuce hadda do at least a six-pack down south, down at the asshole end udda state. Texas Department of Corrections, I'm talking about. Hey, that's what I thought when that judge said six years. I'm going, holy shit, did he say *six?*"

Jack didn't answer as he took his seat. "But get this," Teddy said. "I keep my nose clean—"

"Deuce."

"—and I do some fucked-up job training—"

"Hey, Deuce."

Teddy turned to the big man. "The fuck is so important?"

"How about we trade seats so I don't have to look at them eels."

Teddy swapped positions with the man. Saying, "You believe this guy, Jackie? Say hello to Fredrick Mertts. Does five years inna Ellis Unit and he's afraid of something from a fish tank."

"They won't hurt you," Sandra said. She was looking at this Fredrick Mertts. "Not if you handle them right. Grab them right behind the head, just like a snake."

Mertts shuddered. "I ain't handling no damn snakes with fins."

"So like I was telling you." Teddy again. "I'm thinking I got six to do—and the stench innat place, Jackie, unbelievable—but wit good time and some school, I knock my stretch down to two years. And Mertts had the same release date—you believe that? So, here we are, me and Mertts, back inna world."

"Back breathing free air." Mertts turned his big, zippered head away from the eel tank. "Back sleeping in king-size beds where a man's got room enough to stretch out and have two pillows." He took off his jacket and hung it over the back of his chair. His thick shoulders were covered with light brown hair. It looked as if he were wearing a heavy sweater under the vest. "Hell," Mertts said, "three or four pillows, if a man wants 'em. Feather or foam, take your pick."

Jack watched, trying to figure which one of them would come at him first. "So, Jackie," Teddy said, "the hell you been up to the last two years? The two years my ass was in prison I'm talking about." Teddy was getting louder, his tone taking on a nasty edge. "You know what it's like doing two fucking years in a prison cell, Jackie? Working down inna prison laundry? You think Teddy Deuce had a good time innat place? Go ahead, man, answer the fucking question."

"You have an interesting face," Sandra said.

"You like the face," Teddy said as he turned to her, "the rest udda package'll drive you batshit wit pleasure, if you know what I—hey, I know you."

Sandra struck a pose and smiled.

"No shit, I seen you somewhere. Hey, Jackie, this babe you're hanging wit? I seen her somewhere."

Jack said, "She was just leaving."

Sandra looked at Teddy. "Ever watch television?"

"You hear that, Jackie? She wants to know if Teddy Deuce watches TV. Hey, does a chimp eat bananas?"

"Ever seen a show"—she paused—"called *Double or Nothing?*"

"That's it!" Teddy slapped the table. "I knew I seen you before."

"Number-one syndicated show in five of the fifteen top markets," Sandra said, "among male viewers eighteen to twenty-five."

"I love that show." Teddy beamed. "I ain't just hosing you. I seen it twice since I got out. *Double or Nothing*, that's primo stuff. Hey, I gotta ask you something. That guy Stryker Double, the star udda show, I bet he gets those suits he wears free of charge. Am I right?"

Sandra blinked a couple of times. "Sure . . . I mean, Wardrobe handles everybody on the show."

"Free-of-charge Armani suits." Teddy shook his head slowly. "Man, would I love a gig like that. Unbelievable."

Jack waited for Teddy to look his way. He said, "You didn't come here to talk about TV. What do you want, Teddy?" Telling himself he could stand and swing his chair hard onto the back of Teddy's head. Maybe have a piece of a chair leg still in his hand to use against Fredrick Mertts. Then thinking it would never work, even if he were Stryker Double in a free-of-charge Armani suit.

"Have I ever told you about the last thing me and Jackie here did together?" Teddy leaned toward Sandra. "The last thing my friend Jackie—somebody I loved like a fucking brother, by the way—did for me? A guy I thought was a righteous stand-up? Have I told you about that?"

"Tell me," Sandra said.

"Couple a years ago I had a altercation wit some loser. I handled him, all right? Guy tryda jump me in a motel room, so I defended myself, that's all."

"You beat him to death," Jack said.

Teddy shrugged. "He picked the wrong guy to fuck wit. Case closed." He turned back to Sandra. "So a day or two later I go to Jackie's place. I got a business deal to talk over, we're gonna be partners."

"You came to kill me," Jack said.

Teddy looked at Mertts and pointed his thumb at Jack. "See, Mertts, this is what I been talking about, this guy. He don't talk sense when it comes to Teddy Deuce."

Mertts said, "He thinks about the pigshit instead of the pork chop."

"Fuckin-A right. I guess . . . Anyway, so I go to Jackie's place." Teddy was talking to Sandra again. "I'm gonna offer him a business deal, okay, and what does he do? He takes a fucking pair of pliers and attacks me. He's squeezing my nose like I'm Larry and he's Moe. The motherfucker ruint my face."

Sandra stared at his nose. "It doesn't look too bad. Really, it looks kinda cute."

"It looks like a fucking mongoose tryda chew it off, is what it looks like. The asshole ruint my face. And then what does he do?" Teddy turned and screwed his eyes to Jack's. "You wanna tell her, Jackie? No? Don't feel like talking now, you're all talked out? But you had plenty to say back then—dialing the phone wit your own finger and telling the cops it was Teddy N. Tunstra that nailed the chump inna motel. Your mouth worked just fine onnat call."

"I'll ask you again," Jack said. "What do you want?"

"Hey, Mertts. The skinny jerkola here wants to know what we want. He ain't figured it out yet, he's gotta ask."

The waiter appeared at their table with a bowl of soup. Clouds of steam poured off it. "Soup put in microwave," he said. "Very, very hot now."

"What I want," Teddy said, "is for you to take a ride wit me and Mertts. That's what I want, Jackie."

"Maybe later," Jack said.

Teddy studied his hands, then flipped his gaze on Jack.

"Hey, it ain't like you got a choice."

"Whoa, boys, this is getting too heavy for me." Sandra stood. "I'm outta here." With Jack thinking, Jesus, about time.

As she walked away, Mertts reached to stop her. But Teddy said, "Let her go, Mertts. This is the one we wanna have a party wit." He pointed to Jack. "So what do you say, Jackie? We'll go for a little ride, shunt take long. You gonna walk outta here or do we have to drag your sorry ass out?"

"Depends on where we're going," Jack said. Mertts and Teddy stared at him. He glanced toward the front and saw that Sandra had stopped beside the eel tank.

"Like I said"—Teddy brushed the sleeve of his jacket—"find someplace for you and me to talk about old times."

Jack watched over Mertts's shoulder, trying to keep his eyes from bugging and his jaw from dropping as Sandra plunged both hands in the bubbling tank and grabbed an eel. She pulled it out of the water and held it in front of her as she walked back toward their table.

"Talk about old times," Teddy said, "like when you sent me to prison. That's an old time I got plenty to say about." Teddy reached into the breast pocket of his jacket and pulled out two neatly folded latex gloves. "I got all sorts of things, Jackie, to say about that."

Jack started talking to keep their eyes on him. He said, "I noticed, Teddy, that you don't dress as sharp as you used to. What happened, did prison destroy your taste in clothes?"

"The fuck you saying?" Teddy inspected his jacket. "This is one hundred percent pure silk." He glanced up. "Bitch, what are you doing?"

Sandra stood behind Mertts. She gripped the squirming eel

# 11

*J*ack had a tough time getting to sleep, what with a day full of eel attacks and seventy-mile-an-hour sex with a woman he had never even kissed. Add to that his coming home and finding his house broken into. It didn't take a detective to guess who.

Just in case Teddy and his big friend should come back, Jack retrieved a single-shot .410 out of the hall closet. His grandfather's shotgun. Jack loaded it and placed it next to himself on the bed, where his wife used to lie.

He turned out the light and calmed his mind by remembering an old prosecutor he had known, Howard Bell. Howard was an ex-Navy man who kept his sleeves rolled up to show off his tattoos. He had silver hair and a barrel chest. He smoked Old Golds and operated the best barstool law school in Dallas.

Buy him a scotch and you were admitted. Jack bought him plenty, running a heavy tab at a downtown dump called Boots's, and got to listen Howard Bell's basic theory of law and human behavior: Every case—*every*—was nothing but a search for rot.

Rot, to Howard Bell, was truth. Some might see a beautiful home. Howard poked and prodded for papered-over decay.

Health was a lie, Howard Bell said, but cancer was truth. Ambition was a lie; the truth lay in greed. Love was a lie. Betrayal was truth.

Truth hid in a case like a rattlesnake in your house. You had to keep looking until you found it. Either that, Howard Bell said, or one night you'd walk through a room in the dark and it would find you.

There were many evenings when Jack left Boots's believing that Howard Bell was the wisest man he had ever met.

At six in the morning the phone rang. Jack felt as if he had been asleep for five minutes. He answered anyway, and listened to an old man's voice tell him, "You and me need to talk, bub."

By seven he was sitting in a booth at Greenie's, downstairs from his office, waiting for Norton Luttrall to show. Norton didn't want to talk on the phone. Something about the cops having him wiretapped so they could catch him belching without saying excuse me.

Now Norton shuffled across the linoleum floor at Greenie's, bringing cigar smoke with him like an aura. He wore a crisp white short-sleeve shirt, a black bolo tie, baggy gray pants, and gleaming black wingtips with rubber soles. His straw cowboy hat looked as if it were swallowing his head. He sat down with "All right, you don't have to say it, I was a horse's ass yesterday."

Jack handed him a plastic-coated menu. "Don't worry about it."

"I ain't worried. I'm just telling you." Norton killed his cigar in the pressed-metal ashtray. "You came by, you had some questions, you had a job to do. All right, fine. No reason for me to act the way I did. Even if you did try to put me in jail once."

"I apologize," Jack said. "We were wrong to try to put you in jail."

Norton stared at him, head trembling slightly but dark eyes firm and clear. Jack got ready for another harangue. Norton said, "You mean that?"

"We made a mistake."

The old man removed his hat and set it upside down on the table. Wispy strands of white hair lay across his pale and spotted scalp. "A mistake." He kept his eyes on Jack. "About time somebody owned up to that."

Jack thought about the sleep he was missing. "What was it you wanted to talk to me about, Mr. Luttrall?"

"I just told you. No call for the way I acted yesterday. You said you had some questions for me. Here I am."

A waitress stopped by. Norton ordered coffee and a short stack, butter on the side, and could they heat the syrup before they brought it? The waitress said she could. Norton winked and said, "You make an old man happy."

Jack stirred his coffee, watched it swirl. After a while he said, "Tell me about you and Sherri."

"Sherri." Norton gazed toward a rotating rack full of pies for a few seconds, then came back to Jack. "Lemme ask you something first. You seen her lately?"

"Couple of days ago."

"How'd she look?"

"She looked pretty good."

"She looks pretty good now," Norton said, "how do you think she looked in nineteen sixty-two?"

"I'd say she probably looked very nice."

"No damn probably about it."

Somebody played George Jones on the jukebox, a song about a guy drinking from an Elvis Presley decanter with a Flintstones jelly jar glass. *I pulled the head off Elvis, and filled Fred up to his pelvis.* Jack sang along with the refrain: *Yaba-daba-do, the King is gone, and so are you.* Then he said, "Okay, it's nineteen sixty-two, Sherri's looking very nice. You and her, what's the story?"

Norton chewed his cigar, drank some coffee, and chewed some more. He sat back against the booth and shook his head once. "Tell you one damn thing, that girl could dance. You remember Louie Chick's club on Commerce Street? Not the one on Harry Hines. The one downtown. The hell was the name of that place?"

"The only old club on Commerce I ever heard of was owned by Jack Ruby. You talking about the Carousel?"

"If I was talking about the Carousel, that's what I woulda said. Can we get that straight, me and you? If I say it, I'll mean it. That's my promise to you. Right now I'm talking about Louie Chick's place on Commerce. Big Polish bartender in there named Frank, his wife tried to shoot him one night. Remember that?"

Jack shook his head no.

"The lady found out about Frank fooling around on her. Walked right in, took the gun outta her purse, and started firing. Missed Frank, but she did kill a hell of a lot of liquor. And was Louie Chick pissed, oh my God. Yelling at him, 'You dumb Polack bastard, next time she's shooting at you, stand in front of the cheap stuff.'"

Norton slurped his coffee. "Anyway, make a long story short, that's where me and Sherri got to know each other, Louie Chick's place. She wasn't Louie's headliner, I'll give you that. But she danced, and she took her clothes off while she was dancing, and I watched. Pretty soon I was doing more than that. What I'm saying is, we had our fun for a while. Am I making myself clear?"

Jack nodded.

"You understand what I'm telling you?"

"Plain as day."

Norton was staring at the pie case again. "We carried on for a month or two, maybe, I don't know. Don't ask me. I was married at the time, so I didn't keep no diary."

"Subsequent to your affair," Jack said, slipping into lawyer-speak, "Sherri gave birth to a baby. Your daughter."

Norton sighed and waited a few beats before saying, "My daughter." He was looking past Jack, but his eyes had lost their focus.

"When did you see her last?" Jack asked.

Another pause. "She was just a baby." Jack had to lean forward to hear. "Just a baby, last time I knew anything about her."

"Did you ever meet the people who adopted her?"

Norton twisted his face in annoyance. "Who told you that?"

The waitress set their breakfasts on the table. Norton took knife and fork to his pancakes as if they were trying to escape. The two of them ate without talking until Jack said, "All those years, no letters, no phone calls?"

Norton's voice rose. "What I just said, if you was paying any attention. Which I'm beginning to have my doubts."

"Didn't you want to find out what happened to her?"

Norton kept a pancake pinned down with his fork while he wiped at his mouth with a paper napkin. "Sometimes," he said as he took another bite, "you know all you want to know, even if you don't know everything. That's probably hard for a boy like you to believe, but you'll figure it out one of these days."

Jack spread jelly on his toast. "That's a nice neat little lesson, Mr. Luttrall."

"Pretty good pancakes," Norton said through a mouthful.

"But I'm thinking the only reason you're here right now, the thing that brought you in here this morning to talk to me, is you want to know what I know."

Norton stopped eating. "Go ahead, you got something to say, spit it out. Anything I can't stand, it's a mealy-mouthed son-ofabitch."

Jack took a deep breath and looked across the room, trying to keep a lid on his irritation. Talking to Norton was like having someone poke a finger into your ribs with every other sentence. "You're here to trade information," Jack said. "Something about the case I'm on has hooked you. I don't know what it is. You might be after money. You might want to find out about your daughter. I don't know. But you're hoping that if you give me some information, I'll give you some in return."

Norton sat up straight and put his hands flat on the table. "Well, what do you know. Here's a boy that's figured out the way the world works. Congratulations." The waitress came to refill their coffee cups. Norton turned to her with "Better call the newspaper, hon. We got us a real live genius"—pointing at Jack—"right here amongst us. Kinda makes you want to drop to your knees in awe, don't it?"

Dean Dudley swam out of a deep sleep to hear knocking on his apartment door. Like someone banging on his head with a hammer, and not stopping to rest. He grabbed a pair of boxer shorts from the bedroom floor and pulled them up as he moved toward the noise. Telling himself, If it's a Jehovah's Witness waking me up, then somebody's about to get a copy of *The Watchtower* shoved right up their holy ass. Saying, "You know what time it is, fuckface?" even before he got the door all the way open.

"Inside-out underwear," Ricks Harrison said, looking him over. "Very attractive, Dinky."

Ricks walked past Dean and into the apartment. He was followed by a small pale man and a large dark one. Ricks said, "This is what I don't understand, Dinky. You've married a woman who lives in a beautiful house in North Dallas, and you've still got this . . . how to describe it?" He looked around the room. "This drab little place."

"What do you want?" Dean was thinking how much he'd love to smash something hard into pretty boy's face. Didn't matter what—crowbar, coffee cup, frozen chicken.

Ricks took a seat at the kitchen table and motioned the others to do the same. "Dinky, this is Falo." Ricks pointed at the big man. "He's Samoan, should you be curious. And this"—Ricks laid a hand on the small man's shoulder—"this is Ed. He's my brother-in-law. Please sit down, Dinky, join us. Do you have a brother-in-law?"

"Uh, I don't know." Dean took the fourth chair. "Ricks, what're you doing here, man? You said get you the money on Monday. Right? That was the deal we worked out, you and me."

"In the manner of brother-in-laws everywhere," Ricks said, "Ed is out of work. The unfortunate victim of corporate downsizing. Am I correct on that?"

"Yeah." Ed chewed gum as he nodded. "Laid off." A thin, bat-faced guy with short red hair and a Hawaiian shirt, Ed looked at Dean and said, "Ricks is teaching me the business."

"Ed is very good with numbers," Ricks said. "Would you like a demonstration, Dinky?"

"See, Ricks, I don't understand, man." Dean watched as Ricks nodded at the big Samoan, who got out of his chair. "I mean, we had a deal, right? And everything is on schedule. I'm talking about the money being in the pipeline, okay? I mean, the cash is on the train." The Samoan was standing behind him. Dean said, "Ricks, you gotta believe me."

Ricks smoothed his hair. "Dinky, please, a little quiet while we conduct our demonstration. You ready, Ed? All right, here's the question. Listen carefully, now. Here it is: How many people in this room owe me money?"

Ed seemed to be thinking it over. Dean said, "Ricks, we had a deal, man. And I'm holding up my end. I'm doing every—"

He stopped talking when Ricks reached across the table and, with thumb and forefinger, grabbed the hairs around Dean's left nipple.

"Dinky"—Ricks tugged at the hairs—"if you don't shut up, I'm going to ask Falo to find a pair of scissors and cut your tongue out." Ricks released his grip and looked toward Ed. "Our question again," he said. "How many people in this room owe me money? Ed, the answer, please."

Ed cleared his throat. "Actually, Ricks, the answer is two, 'cause you loaned me a C-note last week that I ain't paid off yet."

From behind Dean the Samoan said, "And I owe you twenty from the other night, Ricks."

Ed nodded. "So the answer is three."

Ricks closed his eyes, rubbed his temple, and sighed. "All

right. I'll rephrase. How many people here owe me money"—he held up a finger—"for wagers they have placed and lost."

Ed said, "Uh, I believe that'd be one, Ricks."

"I'm gonna pay you, Ricks." The words blew out of Dean before he could bottle them up. "No bullshit, man, you'll get your money. You gotta believe me, you—"

Ricks, leaning across the table, had his chest hairs again. "A reminder, Dinky . . . Falo? Scissors?"

Another nod from Ricks and the Samoan reached over Dean's shoulders. His huge hands anchored Dean's wrists to the table. Dean tried to move his arms but might as well have been nailed down. The Samoan breathed through his mouth, right by Dean's ear. He smelled like garlic and hair spray.

Ricks sat back and said, "Do you have a cigarette I could borrow, Ed?"

"Sure thing." Ed pulled a pack of Camels from the front pocket of his Hawaiian shirt, tapped a cigarette free, and offered it. Ricks shook his head. Saying, "Light it for me."

"Ricks," Dean whispered. "Please, man." As Ed struck a match and put it to the cigarette, Dean could feel himself shaking against Falo. "Please," he said again.

"The thing you have to remember, Ed, is that ours is a business like any other." Ricks carefully rolled up his sleeves. "We have bills and obligations just like anybody else. So cash flow is important."

Ed blew smoke toward the ceiling. "I gotcha."

"Now, the sad fact is, some people tend not to pay their bills to us on time. And in that case we have to send them a friendly notice." Ricks used two fingers to motion for the cigarette. "A little reminder that they shouldn't neglect their obligations."

Ed nodded. "Ditto on the I gotcha."

"Dinky," Ricks said, "you having memory problems?"

"Ricks, I—"

"You know the policy. You owe ten K or more, you check in

every day. Just so I know you're still around. Remember that? Dinky, I'm talking to you."

"Come on, man. I overslept. That's all, Ricks. I just slept too long. I was working late last night. Hey, everybody sleeps."

Ricks took the cigarette from Ed and held it upright, like a tiny torch. "It's not something I particularly like to talk about, but I once put one of these out in a fellow's eye. Ed, could you kindly assist Falo by holding Dinky's head still?"

Ed stood. Dean said, "Ricks, don't do this. Please, man, I'm begging you." He couldn't move under the load of Samoan flesh.

Dean heard Ed say, "Excuse me, Falo, I need a little room to work here." The Samoan load shifted. Two hands grabbed two clumps of hair at the back of his head. Ed's voice again: "All set here, Ricks."

The glowing orange tip of the cigarette was inches from Dean's face. The smoke curled into his nose. Tiny whimpers rose out of his throat. The crotch of his boxer shorts turned warm, and a stream of urine ran down one leg.

Ricks stretched farther across the table, and the cigarette left Dean's line of vision. Dean felt fingers at the side of his head, and then something in his left ear—soft but filling the hole.

"There," Ricks said as he relaxed back into his chair. His hands were empty. Dean took a couple of seconds to understand that the unlit end of the Camel was in his ear. Ricks laced his fingers on the table. He said, "That should take about two minutes to burn down to what I like to call the point of influence."

Dean was trying to shake his head, straining against Ed's grip and the bulk of the Samoan. Thrashing his bare feet and banging his knees against the underside of the table. Screaming, "I'll pay you, Ricks. Swear to God, I'll get you the money, every penny. Please, man, don't do this." Twisting his eyes to try to see the burning cigarette, dreading the first bloom of pain at his ear.

Finally, Dean began to cry. Two times he managed to say, "Ricks, I'll pay you." Then his sobs took over.

Ricks leaned toward him, and Dean's ear was free. "Of course you will, Dinky." Ricks flicked the Camel toward the kitchen sink. He smiled, showing Dean a perfect row of white teeth. "Was there ever any doubt?"

They were on their fifth cup of coffee, Jack and Norton Luttrall, in the booth at Greenie's after maybe an hour, practically old pals at this point. Jack still didn't know Norton's angle, but he gave him the highlights of the last few days. Most of them, anyway. He left out the part with him and Sandra on the freeway.

Norton had plenty of questions about Sandra: What did she look like now, what kind of person was she, did she talk much about her past, how come she picked right now to show up in Dallas? And how about this story of growing up in California, what did he know about that? I'm looking into it, Jack said.

Talk of Sandra seemed to make Norton fold his barbs away, except when Jack told about events leading up to his dive into the moving Mustang. "Ain't a bit of that makes any sense," Norton said.

"What are you talking about?"

"You asking that with a straight face?"

"No, I'm laughing my ass off at the thought of being stabbed." Which reminded Jack, his arm hurt. He rubbed it gently. "You have a question about some part of that account?"

"Question ain't the word, bub. It smells like a tin shithouse in August."

Jack waited while Norton found a new cigar in his pocket, unwrapped it, and looked it over like a federal inspector. After a minute or so Norton said, "Thirty years in the bail bond business, how many criminals you think I met?"

"Whatever I say, it's not going to be enough, is it?"

"A man operates a successful bonding agency, he runs into a few lawbreakers. I mean, if he don't, he's outta business. Say the

police stop arresting people, then the bail bondsman's got no customers. Understand what I'm saying?"

Jack gave a thin smile. "I was a prosecutor, remember? Your
customers were my defendants."

"Then I shouldn't have to explain this to you. But maybe you
spent all your time going after innocent people like me—"

"Oh, boy, here we go again."

"—that maybe you never saw any guilty ones. So I'll let you
in on a little secret, bub. Most of your criminals are a bunch of
dumb bastards that don't think past right now. They see something they want, they steal it. They see somebody in their way,
they kill him. Now"—Norton paused to light his cigar, puff a few
times, and study the smoke—"you do have your exceptions."

Jack watched the waitress pour cup number six. "You got
your planners," Norton said. "This boy we're talking about here,
this kidnapper, you want to put it that way, seems like he's working on some kind of plan."

"Seems like," Jack said.

"I mean, here's some sorry sack that wants to grab a girl. All
right, fine. But he follows her around first, figures out where she
goes and what she does. Sneaks into a country club, Christ's sake,
to slice up her unmentionables. Goes to the trouble to put on a
disguise before he comes after her. Then what does he do? Tries
to snatch her in the middle of a busy street? Go ahead, explain
that one to me, I'm listening."

Jack rubbed his face. The coffee buzz felt like a small beehive
in his head. "I'll tell you what else bothers me. Three blasts from
the past."

Norton folded his napkin. "Uh-huh."

"All these people reappearing at the same time. Teddy
Deuce, out of prison. Sandra Danielle, who blows back into
Dallas after thirty-four years. And you, her father, somebody I
never thought I'd see again, here we are having breakfast."

Norton had his hat in his hand. "I'd give it some thought, I

89

was in your boots. Three's a big number for that kind of thing, been my experience." He slid to the end of the booth.

"One person, one time—that's no big deal." Jack shrugged. "Two at once happens every now and then. But three reincarnations, all at the same time and same place, that's either divine intervention or somebody dicking with something."

"Well, tell you what, if I was you"—Norton settled his hat on his head—"I wouldn't believe one damn thing anybody told me."

Jack looked to Norton's eyes but found nothing. "That include you, Mr. Luttrall?"

The old man stood, a little shaky getting up but steady once he got there. "One thing I have to ask about you, bub. How come to make you understand something I always have to tell it to you twice?"

Jack said, "I'm sorry, could you repeat that?"

"Funny guy." Norton puffed his cigar. "I'll give you a tip, bub, not that you deserve it. But I'm gonna do you a favor, don't ask me why. This case here, there's an oddball in the mix. Find out who it is, you're all set."

He started to go. Jack stood and came after him with "Hey, wait a minute." Norton turned. Jack said, "What do you know about this?"

"All I'm saying is, there's a joker in the deck."

"And all I have to is find him. Or her. Then it's case closed."

"Bingo," Norton said.

With Jack thinking, Who the hell says that anymore? "Bingo?"

"B-I-N-G-O," Norton said as he turned and walked away. "Goddamnit, I knew I'd have to say it twice."

# 12

*J*ust what I need, Jack thought after Norton left. One more proud member of the liars' club. But he had to admit that Norton had jarred loose some thoughts. Jack climbed the stairs to the Greenie's Office Building and unlocked his door, phoning Sherri as soon as he got to his desk, telling her he wanted to talk. She said, "Hey, baby, me and Sandra's gonna be lonely this afternoon. Come on over then."

Jack spent the next few hours on the computer and on the phone, trying to put together a picture of Dean Dudley. If you wanted an oddball, Dean seemed like a good bet.

Dean was thirty-two. He had title to a silver 1996 BMW 740i, but not much else that Jack could find. His driving record included a DUI arrest in 1992, and his first marriage ended in divorce five years ago. Personal bankruptcy followed a year later. Dean had contributed to no political candidates, nor was he a graduate of the state's universities. He subscribed to *Penthouse*.

Not exactly a stellar citizen, Jack was thinking, but no Charles Manson, either. He was about to close the file when Mike Tinsley, a friend from the DA's office, called back. "Dean Edward Dudley," Mike Tinsley said, reading from a record. "Just recently completed three years probation for felony theft. Let's see . . ." Jack listened to papers being shuffled. "Here we go, probation officer's report." More shuffling, then: "Looks like, Jack, your boy got lovey-dovey with an older woman in Highland Park who'd just buried her husband. Ended up running off with her car and checkbook. Credit cards, too."

Jack half wished Norton Luttrall was there to spell bingo for him.

That afternoon was warm, muggy, and absolutely still, the sky heavy with a nauseous green tint. Jack was on the road ten minutes when a blinding thunderstorm hit—a pelting roar on the Chevy's roof, the rain coming down so hard his wipers seemed to flail at it.

Traffic crawled as intersections became shallow lakes. Storm sewers overfilled and flowed outward like curbside springs. The radio crackled with lightning static as announcers warned of flash floods from creeks that usually weren't much more than trickles of slime.

Rain often fell on Dallas the way money might drop on some hard-luck bastard who every now and then picked a winner at the track. Not often enough, or regularly enough, and when it did come there was too much, too fast to handle.

It was still pounding when Jack reached the Omerdome. A run from the street to the door left him soaked. "Oh, look at you, baby," Sherri said. She gave him a thick towel and offered to let him use some of Omer's clothes while his dried.

"That's all right," Jack said.

Sherri opened a hall closet and came back with a maroon suit hanging under cleaner's plastic. "This was one of his favorites. I almost had him buried in it. You take it, baby. Omer ain't around to mind."

Jack waved her off. "I'm fine. Where's Sandra?"

"She'll be down in a shake. Then we can all talk, let you give us a status report."

They walked to the kitchen, where Sherri began to mix a drink. She said, "That envelope by the phone's for you." Jack opened it and fanned a stack of hundred-dollar bills with his thumb. "Four days' pay," Sherri said. "How about a cocktail to celebrate?"

"I'll take one," Sandra said, walking in. Wearing a white t-shirt knotted at the midriff and black spandex bicycle shorts. Coming toward Jack with "There he is, *Car and Driver's* man of the year." She put a quick hand on his ass and kept right on going to the refrigerator, where she bent in front of the chrome handle and checked her lipstick. Then she straightened and faced Jack. "You taking me out tonight?"

She gave him a look he remembered, her eyes the two green pools that Stryker Double used to dive into at the end of each show.

There was the banging of a spoon on the counter. Sherri said, "Before you two head for the rut hut, Mr. Jack here said he wanted to talk. So let's do that first."

"You're right." Sandra moved to Sherri and hugged her. "Let's talk."

"Good idea," Sherri said, "and let's get it done quick 'cause I got a party to plan. I'm giving Sandra a big sendoff, baby. You're invited . . . So"—she sipped from her glass and looked at Jack—"who's the fool chasing my baby girl? You got that figured out yet?"

With Jack thinking it probably was an expanding list, what with the big guy she dropped the eel on yesterday. He said, "Tell me about your husband."

"Baby, Omer Plunkett's in the box now. What else is there to tell?"

Sandra squeezed her again. "I think he means Dean."

Sherri squeezed back. "I know that, little girl. I was just having a joke." Then to Jack. "All right, the story of me and Dean . . . I don't know any way of giving this to you delicate, baby. So I'll just lay it straight out. You ever had a time in your life where all your thinking was in your pants?"

Sandra clapped her hands twice and laughed out loud. Jack said, "Does a chimp eat bananas?"

"Sometimes I make things worse by having"—Sherri raised her glass like a toast to Jack—"a little too much to drink. I'll admit it. I don't need to go to any damn meetings or anything. But, hey, sometimes Sherri has a good time and when she thinks she oughta stop she comes to find out the brakes has failed."

Sandra was smiling and singing, *And along came Dean-o.*

"I met Dean a few months after Omer passed. Working on my tan and there he was. Dean, not Omer, baby. He took care of the pool at Preston Bend. First time I saw him he come over to see if I needed Hawaiian Tropic rubbed on my back."

"Wait a minute." Jack straightened and pointed at Sandra. "The country club where somebody sliced up your underwear?"

Sandra made a noise like the *Twilight Zone* theme. "Talk about a place with bad vibes."

"One thing I have to admit," Sherri said. "Dean looks good with his shirt off, I'll give him that. He can talk to a lady, I'll give him that, too." She let out a tired sigh, adding a few years, it seemed to Jack, with just one heavy breath. "Tote all those things up and two weeks later we got married. Tell you the truth, I don't remember too much about it. But I've seen the license and hon, it's right there in black and white. Dean Dudley and Sherri Plunkett, husband and wife."

Jack looked toward the stairs. "Is he here now? I'd like to talk to him."

Sherri shook her head. "Only time Dean shows up is when he needs money."

"Just out of curiosity." Sandra ran her hands through her hair the way she did in her shampoo commercial. "Why are you asking all these questions about Dean?"

Jack thought about the time he shook hands with Dean, and remembered what he could of the guy who stabbed him. Telling himself: Might be, could be. He said, "Maybe Dean's the stalker."

"Dean?" Sandra laughed. "*Dean?* You've got to be kidding me. What I've seen of that moron, he couldn't stalk a snail." Another laugh, looking at Sherri. "You believe this?"

Jack turned to Sherri, half expecting her to demand her money back. But she cocked her head and said, "Something to think about."

"Oh, come on." Sandra leaned both elbows on the kitchen counter, hands over her face. "You can't be serious."

"Well, hon, it can't hurt to check, can it? Mr. Jack's the expert, let him run with it, see what happens." She looked at Jack. "What's on your mind, baby? Tell Sherri what you need."

"Where's Dean now?"

Sandra kept her hands over her face. "This is such a waste of time."

"My guess," Sherri said, "is Dean's out driving that brand-new silver BMW I made the mistake of buying him. Or you'll find him out at the country club. When he worked at Preston Bend? Couldn't stand the place. Now he loves to hang out there and charge everything to Sherri's account."

"What I'd like," Jack said, "I'd like to go upstairs and check his closet a little, maybe poke around anywhere else he keeps his things."

Sherri opened a cabinet above the sink and removed a key ring from a hook. "You think I'd let him live here, baby, in my house? Dean's got his own place. Which I pay the rent on, by the way. Here you go." She tossed the key ring to him. "That'll get you in the front door. Poke around all you damn please."

"I'll go with you." Sandra came to Jack's side. "We'll poke together. And then"—she ran a fingernail along the ridge of his ear—"we'll go out and see what kind of real trouble we can get into."

Jack took the envelope full of money from the counter, folded it, and slid it in his back pocket. He glanced toward the kitchen window. Outside it was pouring.

# 13

"I never thought I'd say this, Deuce. I never thought I'd even *think* it. You know what I mean?"

Teddy Tunstra stared out the restaurant window, watching the afternoon rain fall on Greenville Avenue. "Not one clue, Mertts."

"I mean last night, man. I couldn't sleep. No matter how many pills I take, I'm tossing and turning. Every time I close my eyes I see eels." Mertts shivered. "Ain't no words to describe the horror of it."

"Hey, you think you're pissed?" Teddy turned from the window. "Lookadis, Mertts. This salve, this medicine for the hot soup? It's staining my shirt. The motherfucker that did this, Mertts? That asshole Jack Flippo? He's gonna wish Teddy N. Tunstra the Second wasn't never born."

"But listen to what I'm saying." Mertts leaned forward, the table creaking under his weight. "Maybe it's a good thing I couldn't sleep. 'Cause as bad as it was thinking about them eels, imagine how hairy the dreams mighta been."

"Yo, honey." Teddy was talking to a waitress. "Your manager here? Tell him I wanna see him."

"I musta paced that motel room five hundred times, Deuce. I bet there's a path worn in the rug now. Back and forth, forth and back. The whole time I'm hearing this voice in my head."

"What else is new?"

Mertts stopped talking and rubbed his scar. Teddy watched him, remembering the way the guy had been in prison: Screaming in pain sometimes. Rolling around on the floor, his headaches so bad. Just like Jimmy Cagney in that old movie where he was a gangster who loved his ma.

Some of the other cons watched Mertts throwing his fits and walked away. But Teddy saw an opportunity. He had a friend with a connection in the prison pharmacy, so he cashed in some favors to get Mertts a steady supply of Percodans and Talwins. His payoff: Teddy had one of the biggest, meanest guys in the Ellis Unit at his side, loyal as a dog.

"Hi, I'm Carl." A nervous man wearing a tie stood at their table. "Can I help you?"

"You the manager?" Teddy didn't wait for an answer. "You got a problem inna men's batroom. There's barely enough soap innere to wash my hands."

Carl nodded. "Did you have enough for yourself, sir?"

"That ain't the point, Ace. What if right after I'm done, the guy who comes in is the same guy that's gonna prepare my food? He don't have the soap to do a proper job. So what's he do, he rinses his hands maybe?"

Carl apologized, said he'd look into it personally. "Asshole," Teddy said when he was gone.

Mertts rapped the table top with his big knuckles. "Hear that, Deuce? That's an idea knocking."

Teddy winced. "Is the plate in your head rusted, Mertts? The fuck are you talking about?"

"This is what I'm trying to tell you, man, what come to me last night. Set the scene for you." Mertts made a frame with his fingers. "Here it is: You, Deuce, are on the snore shelf and I'm pacing the room. I'm thinking, soon as Deuce wakes up I bet we go looking for them two that screwed us over in the Chinese restaurant."

"*Looking for* ain't the word. Cutting up into tiny pieces and feeding to turtles inna park, that's the word."

"Maybe we been too hasty in all this. You know, breaking into the wrong house twice. Then letting 'em get the drop on us yesterday."

"Hey, they dint get the drop on me. Not on Teddy Deuce. You're the one went batshit first, Mertts." Teddy flagged a passing waitress. "I gotta die of thirst before I get something to drink here?"

Mertts ran fingers through his curls. "First thing that come to me is this. From now on, we take our sweetass time with this dude Flippo. We wait and we get him how we want him."

"Fucking dead, is how I want him."

"Right, man. Exactly. But we wait till it's the right time and the right place."

Teddy lifted his nose and sniffed. He smelled disinfectant and blue cheese. His chest and neck had second-degree burns. And even with Duff's money his wallet felt thin; getting back at Jack Flippo would be great, but the chase wasn't throwing off any cash.

"So I'm thinking about all this," Mertts said. "I'm pacing the room. Then guess what I seen under the phone. A phone book, man."

"Imagine that."

"But it ain't the same phone book we used before. This one's the business pages, man. It's got businesses in it."

Teddy gazed out the window. "It's gonna fucking rain all day, you know it? You know what that does to the drape of a linen jacket, Mertts?" He studied his coat. "Now I wouldn't be wearing linen onna day like today, except some future fucking dead asshole ruint my hundred percent silk jacket wit hot soup."

"So I go straight to this phone book. I mean, the voice in my head was telling me to get on it like a laser beam." Mertts unfolded a page from his pocket and smoothed it on the table. He pointed to a line he had circled in blue. "Read what it says right there."

"You ever seen eyes this red, Mertts? I try to read something that small, I'll pop a vein and bleed to debt."

"Help you out. It says, Flippo Investigations on East Grand Avenue. The dude's a detective, Deuce, and this is his office. Let's just go stake it out and wait for him to show. Simple as that."

"Let me see that." Teddy studied the page from the phone book. The last time Teddy had seen Jack Flippo, the guy barely had enough scratch for lunch, never mind an office. He must have pulled himself together.

Teddy thought about what would be in an investigator's office. Equipment he could steal, for one. But also files. Information. All sorts of secret shit. Pictures of husbands jumping other people's wives. Maybe something about somebody stealing from where he works. Could be stuff that people thought was dead and gone, finished with. Put it in the right hands, Teddy thought, and it's a commodity. The blackmail proceeds alone could run into the thousands.

"Yo, Mertts," Teddy said. "You feel like breaking into something?"

Jack and Sandra left the Omerdome around four, Jack driving his Chevy, with the address of Dean's apartment on the dash. "Do you really think you're going to find anything?" she asked him. "Like what's he going to do, have a list labeled 'Dean's Kidnapping Plan' on his coffee table?"

"People leave all sorts of stuff lying around."

Traffic was heavy, and so was the rain. The sky was dark enough that some of the streetlights had come on, but Sandra wore sunglasses anyway. Every time she moved, Jack turned to see what she was doing. Thinking, you never knew with this one.

Sandra said, "All right, let's say you hit, three cherries in a line. You walk in and the whole place is full of stuff to convince you Dean's the guy. What then?"

99

"Then I tell the client."

"Straight to Sherri."

"That's right."

"You tell her everything?"

"Everything I can find that has a bearing on the case."

"And you don't go to the police?"

"With what?" Jack looked through a shoebox on the seat between them, searching for a Marty Robbins tape. Or failing that, Merle Haggard. All he could find was a musical tribute to the seventies, which his second ex-wife had given him, her idea of a joke.

Jack shoved the tape in the player and "Disco Inferno" filled the car. "Go to the cops with what?" he said over the music. "Evidence that I nabbed illegally, on a crime somebody hasn't committed yet? I think the best you could hope for would be to spook Dean off his plan."

"That's good." Sandra was disco-dancing in her seat. "I don't think Sherri wants the police in this. She doesn't trust them or something."

At a red light he watched her dance. She was shaking her chest nicely, it seemed to Jack. He said, "You know, for someone who's the target of a stalker and a snatcher, you don't look all that worried."

Sandra stopped, leaned toward Jack, and put her hand on his thigh. She peered at him over the tops of her shades. "If we were in a movie right now? I'd say something like, It's because I'm with you, babe."

The next song came on, "Kung-Fu Fighting." Jack and Sandra looked each other over until the driver behind them leaned on his horn.

Teddy and Mertts listened in the second-floor hallway of the Greenie's Office Building for nearly a minute. Mertts said, "Like a tomb in here."

One door had J. FLIPPO in white lettering. Teddy gave it three knocks, waited, then three more. "Nothing," he said.

Mertts, using the vise grips they had bought from the True Value Hardware next door, worked on the dead bolt. It took thirty seconds.

"Assistant warden down at Ellis Unit had a better office than this," Teddy said as he walked in. "Asshole don't even have a TV in here."

Mertts sank onto the couch. Teddy sized up the copier and the fax machine, wondering what they would bring him at a pawnshop. Then he moved to the desk and opened the first folder he saw. He shuffled through four or five typewritten pages before coming to an eight-by-ten, black-and-white photograph of a woman with thick hair and a fetching smile.

"Shit on a stick, Mertts, look at this." Teddy held the picture for him to see. "It's the bitch that eeled you."

# 14

Dean's apartment, in a small brick complex near Cole and Fitzhugh named Uptown Manor, looked like a college sophomore's. Neon beer signs on the wall, unwashed dishes in the sink, dirty socks on the floor. Furniture from Rent-A-Center. A bong on one shelf. Pro football posters and girlie magazine pinups in the bedroom.

Jack said, "Put on a Led Zeppelin tape and I'll time-trip back twenty years."

Sandra studied a print tacked to the living room wall, dogs playing poker. "Sherri must have been one lonely chick when she met this guy."

Jack started in the kitchen and progressed to the living room, checking cabinets and shelves. Sandra waited on the couch, reading a magazine. Jack moved to the bedroom. In its drawers and closet he found the clutter of a single man's life and not much else. No familiar-looking knives, no nylon-stocking mask. Twenty minutes after they had arrived he said, "There's nothing here. I'm ready to go."

"Told you." Sandra put her magazine on a coffee table, next to a stack of receipts and some scraps of paper. "Look at all this stuff. What a slob." She went to the front door and walked out.

Jack lagged behind, wondering how he'd missed the papers

in his first sweep of the room. Another sign of getting old, he thought as he bent to pick them up.

One of them caught his eye: a receipt for $500 paid to the Texan Trail Motor Inn on Fort Worth Avenue. An odd part of town for a guy like Dean. Jack slipped it into his pocket as he left.

The rain had stopped. Sandra stood by Jack's car in the puddled parking lot, looking at the clearing sky. The wind pushed the hair back from her face. She was smiling. "I knew this would happen," she said. "This is perfect."

Jack leaned against the roof of the Chevy. "Perfect for what?"

"You know a place called Lake Grapevine?"

"Sure."

"Know how to get there?"

"It's about a half-hour from here."

"Good." Her smile broadened. "I called out there today and rented us a boat."

The worst fucking day of my life, Dean Dudley said to himself. First Ricks Harrison drops by to stick an unfiltered Camel in his ear. Then Dean tries to unwind by going out to Preston Bend Country Club, where he gets into a poker game in the bar and drops almost five hundred dollars.

Dean unlocked his apartment, kicked his shoes off as he crossed the living room, and went to the refrigerator. "Un-god-damn-believable," he said when he opened the door. No beer. He talked to the walls. "What the hell else can happen?"

He got his answer with a knock at the door. From outside someone called, "Mr. Dudley? You in there? Mr. Dudley?" He recognized the voice—Mrs. Roney, the landlady, probably there to complain that he'd parked his car across two spaces again. He kept telling her that was the only way to treat a Beemer if you wanted to cut down on door dings. Her reply was the same every time: Move it in ten minutes or I'm calling my boy. She meant her son, Randy, who owned a wrecker service.

Mrs. Roney was five feet tall, couple hundred pounds, the widow of a Dallas police sergeant. She spent a lot of her time at her window watching the world, keeping track of who came and went. Mrs. Roney couldn't hear much, but her eyes didn't miss a thing.

She usually wore a pink robe and knockoff-brand running shoes, which was how she looked when Dean opened his door. "You had some visitors today." She peered at him through glasses with rhinestoned cat's-eye frames.

Dean thought of Ricks and his two pals, Ed and the fat Samoan. "Early this morning? Business partners, Mrs. Roney. We got some deals we needed to work out the financing on."

"I don't mean them. I'm talking about the man and the woman, left about a half-hour ago."

Dean took a few seconds. "Now . . . who?"

"I knew you weren't here, 'cause I saw you leave this morning. That's why I watched these two. They let themselves in with a key, stayed about twenty minutes."

He remembered Sherri had a key. "The lady," Dean said, "she have a big pile of blonde hair?"

"Did she have *what?*" Mrs. Roney was blinking. "Big piles around her?"

Dean was close to shouting. "Was this lady you saw about fifty with blonde hair?"

Mrs. Roney shook her head. "Not that old. Dark hair. Dressed like some tart on the street."

Dean looked over his shoulder at the apartment, see if there was something missing or anything left behind. He tried to remember if he'd gotten drunk and invited somebody over, maybe giving them an extra key. Telling them, hey, come visit whenever you feel like it.

"I can't stand out here all night." Mrs. Roney pushed a liver-spotted hand his way. "You want this or not?"

Dean took a small piece of paper from her. "What's this?"

"I got the license number of the car they were in and called Randy." She was waddling away now, her back to him. "Randy knows how to check those things. Had the name to me in ten minutes."

Dean stared at the crabbed handwriting, making out the letters one by one. Then thinking, Who the fuck is Jackson A. Flippo? He was on his couch, about to turn on the TV, when it hit him like a smack in the head. Captain Flying Dickhead was way, way too close.

There was a light chop on the lake and a sunset of turquoise and pink. Jack stood at the helm of a twenty-foot fiberglass ski boat, steering past the jetty of a marina. The costar of the megahit *Double or Nothing* was handing him a cold beer she'd just pulled from the cooler.

Jack could see a few sailboats over near the dam. To his left, a couple of men fished from an aluminum skiff in a grassy inlet. Toward the far shore, a cabin cruiser caught a shaft of sunlight and shone luminous white. He turned his boat toward open water. Before them, for miles it looked like, the storm had swept the lake free.

Their boat had a big Johnson 150-horse that answered with a nice muscular roar when Jack gave it gas. Sandra ran a hand under his shirt. The faster the boat went, the faster her hands moved. When he had it past half-throttle she began to pull off her own clothes.

She was naked as she opened the windshield pass-through and stepped onto the bow deck, kneeling up there like some kind of nautical wet-dream hood ornament. Jack eased off the engine, worried that she'd be tossed off. Sandra flipped over, facing him as she leaned on both elbows, and called, "Come on up."

He cut the throttle and turned for the anchor. "No!" she cried from the deck, not happy. "What are you doing? Keep it going."

Jack looked at Sandra, at the shore, then at Sandra again. She said, "Keep it going. Come on, hurry up." She put one hand between her legs. "Or I'll start without you."

He studied the closest land, a wooded finger curling around a cove, maybe a quarter-mile away. Sandra's hand was moving. "Here I go, baby. You're gonna miss a party. . . . Having a wonderful time, wish you were here."

Jack started the boat forward and turned it toward the open part of the lake. Speed was about five knots, he guessed—how should he know, who the hell was he, Barnacle Bill? "Things are beginning to happen without you," Sandra said.

He had his clothes off and was on the deck next to Sandra, letting his tongue follow where her fingers had led, when she stopped. "What's the matter?" he asked.

"We're not going fast enough."

"We aren't?"

"I'm talking about the boat. Faster."

He stepped back through the windshield and pushed the throttle another half-inch or so, doubling the speed. That seemed to do it for Sandra. She grabbed him as he crawled back onto the deck and said, "Now. Right now."

Jack had meant to keep a steady watch on which way the boat was heading. He forgot. By the time he looked up it had turned and was about fifty yards from the curling wooded peninsula. Jack said, "Jesus, I gotta turn us around."

Sandra squeezed him with her arms and legs. "You're not going anywhere."

They cleared the end of the peninsula by ten feet and cruised into the cove just as Jack was done. Sandra pulled at his back and pushed hard against him. She let out a cry that carried across the water to a thicket of reeds. Jack watched a flock of blackbirds lift off and fly away squawking, like jungle birds in a Tarzan movie when Johnny Weissmuller would do his yodel.

# 15

The cove was about a hundred yards across, with scrub woods thick along the shore. In the soft dusk Jack and Sandra had it to themselves. They lay on the gently bobbing deck—engine off now, boat anchored, clothes on—and watched as swallows darted after bugs. High above were the lights of jets making slow, arcing approaches to DFW Airport.

Sandra tracked one airplane with her finger and said, "I'm going back to L.A. in a few days. Why don't you come with me?"

Jack raised himself on an elbow. "Can you get me tickets to *Love Connection?*"

"You go away for more than a couple of months and they forget about you. Call your agent and it's like, Sandra who? Next thing you know, you own a thriving career as a waitress."

Jack went to the cooler and grabbed two more beers. "When do you start shooting your show again? The crooks in South Florida have got to be running wild about now, what with the fishing detective on vacation."

Sandra sighed. "I had a relationship with Chuck Elston."

She said it as if Jack was supposed to know the name. He said, "Not *the* Chuck Elston."

"The producer of *Double or Nothing.*"

"Of course."

"It went south." She shrugged. "I'm not happy about it. But it happens, you know."

107

Jack opened her beer, then his. "Yes, I do."

"So they paid me off and dropped me from the show."

"Just like that? The cocktail waitress with the bedroom eyes mysteriously vanishes?"

"It wasn't even that good. My role was just, like, gone. When he told me it was going to happen? I said, 'Chuck, do it right. I mean, give me a good script to ride out on. Have me killed, let Stryker Double track down the murderer.'"

"I can see it. He's devastated, but he's working through his grief."

"Exactly. With lots of flashbacks on good times with me."

"A very special episode of *Double or Nothing*."

"So I tell all this to Chuck. He nods and he says, 'I've been thinking about knocking off somebody close to Stryker next season.' I say, 'All right, let's do it.' Then he gives me this look, this biggest-prick-in-the-world face, right? And he says, 'But you're not the actress to pull it off, babe.'"

She took a swallow of beer. A fat yellow moon was rising out of the trees behind her. "I'm like, hey, Chuck? Go fuck yourself, I can act with anybody. *Anybody*, okay? He goes, 'Oh, yeah? Let me see you cry. Right now, right here.'" She gazed across the water. "You should have seen his face."

Jack flashed on an image of his second ex-wife. He remembered the way she would look at him, a look that could have told him everything he needed to know if he hadn't turned away each time.

"Chuck Elston, big shit producer, right?" Sandra talking. "He's telling me, 'You cry and I'll count the tears.' He says, 'Give me ninety-six tears, and you can keep the part.'"

"I didn't know you could count tears. I thought they sort of streamed down together."

"The worst thing? I did it. I was so desperate, and I was so mad, I really did start to cry. Real tears. Just to show him I could. They're running down my face and I go, Is that enough for you, Chuck? He goes, well, that's one, and that's two and that's three . . . "

Jack watched her raise three fingers, one at a time.

"Piece of shit way to get dumped, you know it?" She shook her head. "And the worst thing? Blindsided me like a truck, whammo."

Weak waves lapped at the hull of the boat. Jack thought about big nasty surprises, how they shouldn't happen. Not if you asked all the questions, not if you paid attention. You only had to be alert for the signs: the spot on the skin, the smoke on the wind, the noise at the window, the unreturned kiss. See it coming, that was the trick.

"Anyway, I'm tired of talking about the bad old days," Sandra said. "Let's stop talking and do what we did before."

It flipped a switch within Dean, this combo of Ricks Harrison throwing a fat Samoan on him and Captain Flying Dickhead breathing down his neck. Panic raced through him as he sped along Fort Worth Avenue with night falling.

The cowboy on the sign outside the Texan Trail Motor Inn was missing his head, a problem with the neon. Dean squealed a turn by the sign and gunned his silver BMW up the hill, driving fast, passing the motel's shabby rooms and circling around back.

He parked in the unpaved lot and hurried from the car, nearly falling over the concrete-and-rock wall that bordered the front of the apartments. The wall was knee-high, like something to keep out dwarfs.

Dean took the stairs two at a time, then unlocked the door to apartment number 4. The air inside hung stale and warm. He could still smell the dead squirrels. Dean turned on the window-unit air conditioner. It lagged and sputtered, dimming the ceiling light as it tried to start, finally settling into a rattling hum.

His new tools from Sears were on the kitchen counter next to a couple of legs-up roaches. Dean talked to himself. Saying,

What the fuck is happening, have to get this ready, have to pull the trigger on this thing right away, too much pressure, too many walls closing in.

He felt like a gas leak looking for a match.

Dean began working, moving as fast as he could. He cut wood, he hammered nails, he connected chains, he covered the walls. It took an hour, maybe two, maybe four, he wasn't sure.

The hard work calmed him some. When he was finished he stepped back, still breathing hard, and took it all in. The sight of it soothed him even more. Not bad for a first-timer, he told himself. For a rookie, it was a pretty damn good torture chamber.

On the way back from the lake Jack had told Sandra she should stay somewhere else. He said his house might not be a good bet because who knew if Teddy and Mertts might come back. But a hotel would work. At the front door of the Omerdome he told her, "Look, what if it *is* Dean who's trying to grab you? Why sleep in a house that he can walk right into?"

"It's not him." She laughed. "I mean, no way."

"It could be him, it could be anybody. You don't know."

She took his hand. "Why don't you stay here and protect me?"

They moved inside the house. "Nothing I'd like better," Jack said. "But I've got some work to do."

"All right, look. If it'll make you feel any better, I'll change the code on the burglar alarm. Okay? Safe enough for you?"

Jack glanced around. "Want me to check the rooms?"

"You try to look in every closet and under every bed in this place you'll be here three hours." Sandra touched his cheek. "I'll be fine, okay? Go on and do what you need to do."

When he was gone Sandra locked the front door behind her. She heard Jack's car start, then went upstairs. Sherri's door was shut. Sandra knocked twice with one finger, opened the door, and leaned in, peering into the gauzy light from the hallway.

Sherri was in bed, her black sleep mask on, with a five-cocktail snore going.

In her own room Sandra undressed and tried to do a few stretching exercises, but fatigue was pulling her down. She showered, put on a silk nightgown, and brushed her hair. On TV, Mary Tyler Moore and Dick Van Dyke were saying good night. They pecked a kiss to each other and jumped into separate beds. Sandra turned off the TV and the lights, and drifted easily into sleep.

When she awoke the green figures on her digital bedside clock said 1:10 A.M. The house was quiet.

She tried to go back to sleep but couldn't keep her eyes shut. Sandra lay in the dark with a growing sense that someone else was in the room.

"Who's there?" she said. No answer. She reached for the lamp and switched it on.

Dean Dudley stood at the foot of her bed, smiling. "Party time," he said.

# 16

After Jack left the Omerdome he used his car phone to call home and check his messages: A repair company wanted to put aluminum siding on his house, absolutely free. Also, Norton Luttrall was calling to ask, "You find the oddball yet?"

He phoned Norton back. Telling him, I've got some nosing around to do, why don't you come with me and we can talk? Norton said, Maybe, and hung up. Jack took that for a yes, and half an hour later they were side by side in Jack's car, with Norton going hard on his cigar.

"I got a feeling about this guy," Jack said. "This Dean Dudley. He's about the same size as the one who stabbed me. He's got a prior. The one time I saw him and Sherri together, they weren't exactly lovey-dovey. Man, he looks good for it."

Norton rubbed the bridge of his nose and turned to Jack. "All that sniffing around, and he's the one you smell, huh?"

The car was filling with cigar smoke. With Jack thinking, Who could smell a damn thing now? He pressed two buttons and dropped the rear windows halfway. "You don't sound convinced. What do you think about it?"

"The hell's it matter what I think? You're the one that's supposed to solve all this, what do you care about some old man's theory?"

"Just asking, trying to keep up my end of the conversation."

"Come up with your own goddamn stuff. You're the one getting paid for it."

Jack was starting to wonder if it was worth putting up with Norton to find out what he was willing to tell, which so far hadn't been much. They rode in silence until Norton said, "You seeing a lot of the girl?"

Been seeing all of her, Jack thought. "That's part of the job."

"You like her?"

"I'm not close to making you father of the bride, if that's what you mean. But we get along."

"Bet you do, bub."

Jack let that one float out the back windows with the smoke. He drove toward downtown on R.L. Thornton. Norton seemed to be staring at the skyline. After a while he said, "Tell me something."

Jack waited, then said, "Any particular topic?"

"Back when you and the DA was trying to lock me up on a bogus charge—"

"Oh, man, not again."

"—I know you found out your little bastard snitch was lying. But I want to tell me how you found out."

Jack changed lanes so that he could head west when the freeway forked. He took a big breath and let it out. "You want to know what, now?"

"Jesus Christ, what is it with you? Everything twice."

Jack waved his hand. "All right, I heard you." Another breath. "All right." He had to think of what to tell and how to tell it. In the years since it happened he had not talked about it once.

Norton said, "How about doing it before I die of old age."

"Okay. Darden Ellis, Duh-duh-Darden," Jack said, "claimed to be an eyewitness to your torching of an apartment complex."

"Lying little sack of pus."

"That was pretty much our case—Darden. We might have

had some circumstantial stuff. I seem to recall some tie between you and the owner of the complex—"

"Bobby Fountain. He's dead now, his girlfriend shot him."

"—but Darden was the linchpin." Jack drove over the bridge. Below them, the wide space between the levees was nothing but black, as if a real river were down there, instead of mudflats and a drainage ditch. The only time the Trinity looked good was when you couldn't see it.

"Two weeks before trial," Jack said, "I got a tip. Anonymous caller. When Darden was supposed to have seen you set this fire? Tipster said he was actually in Oklahoma."

He remembered telling Vanessa Ingram about it that night. They were in her bed, the veteran lead prosecutor and her fresh-faced assistant, doing a little postcoital trial strategy, when Jack mentioned the call. Who cares, she said, Oklahoma's close. Darden could have been there and here, too, on the same night. Sometimes, she told Jack, there was such a thing as too much information. This was her case to prosecute, her road back, her only hope. What was he trying to do, destroy her last chance? Throw that so-called tip in the trash, Vanessa Ingram said. Lose it.

Jack didn't do that. He began making calls to the Oklahoma state police and to each county sheriff's office, looking for Darden Ellis's footprints. He did it without reservation, with never a second's doubt. He did it because that was what he did. For twelve days he found nothing.

The morning before the trial was to start Jack walked into his office and found a phone message, a rectangular pink gash on his desk's swelling of white paper. The sheriff of Pushmataha County, Oklahoma, had called.

One of my deputies, the sheriff said when Jack phoned, told me you was looking for records on somebody named Darden Ellis. There was a rustle of paper over the phone line, then the sheriff saying, We held him in our jail overnight on a drunk and

114

disorderly on, let's see, on twenty-one June of this year.

Jack opened his file and paged to the fire department report on the arson Darden claimed he witnessed. He stared at the date, looked away, and stared again: June 21.

Of course I'm sure, the sheriff said when Jack asked him to verify it. And why was Jack getting so excited, he wanted to know. Jack told him it was a very important disclosure, that it could change the entire course of a felony trial.

Hell, the sheriff said, it wasn't a month ago I gave this same information to someone in your office. You what? Jack said.

I got her name right here, the sheriff told him. More rustling of paper. Then the sheriff asking: You know a Vanessa Ingram?

Five minutes later Jack confronted her in her office. She began to yell at him, You bastard, you fucking asshole, sneaking around behind my back, why didn't you dig me a fucking grave while you were at it? She came at him, clawing and swinging. An investigator named Lloyd Boswick, who had come to see what all the noise was about, had to pull her off him.

While Lloyd tried to calm her, Jack wiped blood from the scratches on his face. Then he gathered his files and prepared to go into Johnny Hector's office and tell the district attorney of Dallas County why they now had to ask for a dismissal of all charges against Norton Luttrall.

One glance back gave Jack his most vivid memory of Vanessa Ingram: still fighting against Lloyd's arms to get at him, her face twisted in rage, her eyes burning holes in his.

In the car Norton said again, "So how'd you find out?"

Jack blinked hard and pulled himself back to the present. "I told you, we got a phone call."

"I heard there was more to it than that."

"If you heard about it, then why are you asking me?"

No answer from Norton. Jack took the Sylvan exit, stopped at a light, and turned to the old man. "Ask you right now," Jack said. "You set that fire?"

Norton pulled on his cigar, the end glowing bright orange. "Not in this world."

"But you set plenty of others."

"If I did, they all deserved to be set."

"How many people did you kill?"

"Only the ones that had it coming."

"Like who?"

Norton gave him a long look, then turned away. "Time to stop asking questions."

The neon cowboy was still headless when they reached the Texan Trail Motor Inn. Inside the office the desk clerk was picking a pimple and reading a martial arts magazine.

Jack flashed his receipt from Dean's place. The clerk put down his magazine long enough to look at it and say, "That's for all four units up the hill, around back."

Every light was off as Jack parked in the lot in front of the apartments. He took a flashlight from his glove box and told Norton, "Let's get curious."

Jack played the spot over a low rock wall and a pile of old scrap lumber. Norton gazed at the building, its white stucco milky in the moonlight. "This one's been around a while," Norton said.

"Almost as old as you." Jack shined his flashlight through cloudy windows of the two downstairs units. They looked empty except for a few pieces of shabby furniture. Same with unit 3 upstairs.

Number 4 was the only one with its curtains closed. Jack did thirty seconds of work with a metal shim from his wallet and the front door popped open. He reached around the corner to the inside to find a switch. A sixty-watt bare bulb hanging from the ceiling showed them the place.

Jack checked around the front room: a sagging couch, stained walls, and a foul smell. Norton had gone to the bedroom.

Jack heard him say, "Hey, bub, you're not gonna believe this."

Then telling Jack as he walked in, "Think you dialed a win-ner with this one."

Quilts had been nailed to the walls. All of them must have come from the children's department of the bedding store. Donald Duck, Mickey Mouse, Batman, and the Mighty Morphin Power Rangers stared down from the walls.

Norton poked one quilt with a finger. "The hell's this, insu-lation?"

"Keeps your victim's screams from being heard," Jack said.

The only furniture in the room was the bed. On its mattress lay a sheet of plywood. Two sets of handcuffs had been secured to it, each with a bolt through the connecting chain. Jack picked up one of the cuffs. "For the hands, and for the feet."

"I got eyes, bub." Norton went to the window, raised it, and stuck his head out. "Don't see stairs or a fire escape or nothing. That's a long jump down, too. Where was the code inspector when they put this thing up?" He pulled his head back in and looked at the handcuffs again. "Jesus Christ, this bastard's a sicko. . . . I'll wait in the front."

Jack saw a gray metal toolbox in one corner. Nothing special inside it: pliers, screwdrivers, a hammer, a file, wrenches, and a pair of long-handled bolt cutters. Back in the front room he found Norton opening and shutting a connecting door to the next apartment.

"In case you want to visit your neighbors," Norton said, rap-ping the door with two knuckles. "Maybe drop in and borrow a few manacles."

Jack gave the place one last look and said, "All right, I think I'm done here."

Norton closed the connecting door. "So what's your next step?"

"I'm thinking that over right now." He had his hand on the front doorknob. "Let's go."

"Tell you what I'd do, I was you." Norton pointed at Jack with his cigar. "I'd find the little fruit that put this thing together—what'd you say his name was? Dean?—and I'd bounce him off the wall a few times. After that I'd burn this sonofabitch building down. Then I'd declare the case closed, pick up what's owed me, and go off with my sweetheart, hand in hand with the music playing. That's what I'd do."

Jack shook his head. Thinking, Dimwit Dean worked all this out by himself? Hard to believe. "Too much I still don't know," he said. "But thanks for the advice."

"Why the hell you want to know anything else?" Norton was shouting at him. "Everything you need to know is in the room with the cartoons on the walls. What is it with you? Don't you know when to stop? Christ, bub, don't you ever learn?"

"Party time," Dean said again from the foot of Sandra's bed. He stepped closer.

"Jesus, Dean, you scared the shit out of me." Sandra sat up against her pillows. "What are you doing here? Get out."

"You're going to come with me." He moved toward her as he talked.

"Like hell I am."

"We're leaving now. I got a cozy place for you to hang out in. A cute little motel room."

"Get away from me."

"No chance." He was beside her now, bending down, his thumbs together but his fingers spread, pushing them toward her throat. "It's just you and me, now."

Sandra kept her eyes on Dean as she reached for the bedside table, groping for the phone. Dean came lower, his face only two feet from hers, his fingers encircling her throat. All Sandra's hand could find was the clock radio. She gripped it, then smashed it against the side of Dean's head.

He made a garbled noise and reeled backward, clutching his

ear. Sandra got out of bed, unplugged the radio, and stood with it in her right hand. With her left she motioned Dean toward her. "Come on, asshole, you want another taste of this?"

Dean was hunched over, pulling his hand from his ear and staring at the blood on his fingers. "What'd you do that for?" He sounded as if he were about to cry. "I was just playing around."

Sandra tossed the radio onto the bed. "You dumb bastard. What if she wakes up and comes in? I mean, think about it, if you can think, which I'm beginning to doubt."

"Okay, I'm sorry, all right?"

"What if she wakes up, what if she tiptoes down the hall? Did you think about that before you pulled this stupid trick?"

Dean sagged and looked at the floor. "No," he said quietly.

"Well, let me do your thinking for you, Dean. What if we're in here talking about what we're going to do, and Sherri overhears every word of it? What happens then?"

Dean didn't answer.

"Here's what happens," Sandra said. "Two hundred thousand dollars goes down the drain."

# 17

Sandra said, "I've been keeping our friend Jack busy. I'd like to know what you've been doing?"

"Got the motel room good to go. It's primo perfecto. You should see it."

"I will see it, Dean. Or have you forgotten?"

"How come I can't open my mouth without you busting my chops? All I'm trying tell you is it's time to rock and roll."

They had left Sherri's house, and now were in the silver BMW 740i in the parking lot of a twenty-four-hour Whataburger, with Dean putting away a double-meat, double-cheese. "That's one reason I came to see you," he said with his mouth full, "to let you know it's time to get this show on the road."

"Save your breath."

"The other is, whew, don't know how to put this exactly, but something weird happened today." He swallowed, then shoved some french fries in. "Don't get pissed, all right? I'm not saying it's your fault. But that dude that's supposed to be with you? The detective dude? Get this. He came in my apartment while I wasn't there."

She rolled her gaze over him. "So?"

"So? *So?* This guy, you said he wasn't gonna do anything, and now he's on me like white on rice. How're we supposed to pull something off with this wackpack breathing down my neck? You said he was never gonna get that close. Remember? You said—"

"Dean, get a grip."

"—that he was supposed to make Sherri think that some-body really was trying to grab you, and that's all. Remember that? You said that was the only reason this dude was hanging, to make Sherri think it was real. You kept going, 'Dean, don't worry.' Hey, he's walking around my apartment now? Bet your butt I'm worried."

"Calm down for a minute. Try to listen to what I'm saying. This was good for you, Dean."

"Yeah, I'm sure."

"I was with him every step of the way. He didn't find any-thing. He's got nothing to put you in this. You're off his list, he told me so."

"He told you that?"

"He said it a couple of times. Come on, are you listening to me? He doesn't know what's going on, I'm taking care of that."

Dean stared at her in the orange light from the Whataburger sign. Wondering for a few seconds why he'd ever gotten involved with someone like this. Then remembering: Oh, yeah—money. "The thing is, how do we know what he's gonna do? I mean, who thought he'd dive into your car the other night and fuck up the whole wad? Who knew, huh?"

Sandra tossed her hair. "Look, it worked out. It was a show, all right? A little performance to set everybody up, and it worked fine. Too bad the cops got involved, but it turned out okay. Even though you screwed it up, Dean."

"No fucking way, babe. I did exactly what we said. I got you in the car, I drove off. But then that crazy dude has to go and dive in."

Sandra shook her head. "One small detail you're missing. You drove the wrong way. You were supposed to drive *away* from him, not toward him."

With Dean almost shouting, "But that's the way the car was pointed."

He watched Sandra giving him a tight smile he had learned to hate. Then she said, "That, Dean dipshit, is why they make them with steering wheels."

Dean squeezed his head between his palms, trying to keep himself from blasting apart. "You know, it really pisses me off when you talk to me that way."

She paused. Asking nicely, "What way?"

"Like I'm one of the dumbest pieces of crap you ever met."

Sandra looked away. "Well . . . I'm sorry. I'm sorry I said that. That was wrong. Because that's not the way I really feel."

He closed his eyes and nodded. "It's okay, man."

"The way I really feel"—she turned to him—"is that you are *the* dumbest piece of crap I ever met. How's that?"

Dean made a fist and almost punched her, wanted as bad as he'd ever wanted anything to put it right into those capped teeth of hers. He had to get out of the car to keep from doing it, had to walk around the parking lot for a couple of minutes, talking to himself.

When he got back into the Beemer he said, "Okay, you want to be that way? Fine. I don't give a rat. But listen. We need to do this right now. Everything's ready, so let's do it before this dude figures out anything else. Plus, I need money fast. I need it, like, last week. The way most people need air? That's the way I need this money, so let's roll."

The tight smile again. She said, "Who's planning this thing, me or you?"

"Come on, we both are."

"No, we're not. I am. I'm in charge. I'll tell you when it's time to move. Because I'm the only one who has the brains to pull it off."

For once Dean kept his mouth shut, not arguing with her. "Are we through talking now?" he asked her. "'Cause I got some things I need to do."

*     *     *

The smell of cedar always made Norton Luttrall think of his mother. Lilla Luttrall had kept her clothes in a cedar closet. Norton breathed deeply and flew back sixty-five years: For an instant he was a little boy in a small South Texas town, being pulled close into his mother's skirts.

Pain in his back pushed memory aside, made him into an old man again. He was on his knees in his spare bedroom—the one his wife used as a sewing room before she died—leaning into an open cedar chest. He moved his hand blindly through blankets and sweaters to the bottom of the chest, where he found the packet he wanted.

It was wrapped in brown paper and tied with twine. Norton carried it to his kitchen and cut the twine with a carving knife. The stiff, dry paper crackled and resisted as he unfolded it. Inside were some photographs and a gold heart-shaped locket. Norton's hands trembled as he opened the locket and saw the small curl of fine, light brown hair.

He lingered over the photographs for a minute or two, until he could stand it no longer. Norton rewrapped the package, using fresh paper and new twine, then reburied it at the bottom of the cedar chest.

Norton returned to his kitchen table and began to write with a ballpoint pen on a lined tablet:

> Alright, Bub . . . If you are reading this things have
> taken a turn for the bad. What I'm about to do after I finish
> this letter may not work but I feel I must try so if I am not
> around to explain things to you then this letter will do it for
> me. I know you will keep looking for an explanation because
> that's the kind of dumb bastard you are. You might want to
> ask me why I didn't tell you all of this to begin with, that's a
> fair question. I'm sorry I couldn't and here's why.

It took him another half-hour of writing to finish the note. He put it in an envelope, and sealed it. On the front he printed

DELIVER TO MR. JACK FLIPPO and leaned it against a water glass atop the table. Anyone coming to sort through his possessions would be sure to find it.

Then Norton began to load his car.

Jack parked at the end of his block. Three-fifteen in the morning, full moon, the street and sidewalks empty with the wind kicking up. He cut through a neighbor's yard to the puddled alley and walked to his own house.

His back yard was an unmown rectangle bordered by a chain-link fence. A vegetable garden started in March had been given over to weeds. Two t-shirts flapped from a clothesline, where they had hung for a week or two. A single patio chair, toppled by a storm last month, still lay on its side.

He jumped the fence, moved quickly to his back door, and ran his fingers along the top. The small, clear piece of tape he had stuck there was still in place. He went to each window and found tape for each one. Same for the front door. Unless someone had come down the chimney or burrowed up through the floor, there was no one inside.

Jack's house was a two-bedroom, two-bath cottage for which he and Sally signed the mortgage the week after they were married. She had spent the first few months there decorating it, going for warm over expensive: lots of pillows, a quilt on the couch, curtains, throw rugs, some paintings by a friend. Fresh-cut flowers always stood aslant in a wide-mouthed purple vase on a table by the front door.

Some of it—the quilt, the paintings—she took with her when she left. Some of it Jack gave to Goodwill because he didn't like looking at it. There hadn't been flowers in the house for months. Matching hand towels ceased to hang in the bathrooms. Fresh fruit never ripened on the kitchen windowsill anymore. The place was clean but barren. It had the feel of a midwestern factory town after the factory had moved to Malaysia.

Jack stripped to his underwear and crawled into bed. The last thing he did before he fell asleep was reach to his left, the way he used to lay his hand on his wife's bare thigh. This time his fingers rested on the loaded .410 shotgun beside him.

His hand was still on it when he awakened to the noise. Jack blinked hard against the dark but lay still, listening for another sound, not sure if he'd dreamed the first one.

Then he heard the creak of a loose floorboard somewhere in the front of the house. Jack was out of bed, his feet bare on the hardwood, shotgun cold in his hands. Cocking the gun, he stepped into the doorway of his bedroom and looked up the hallway toward the living room.

He saw the rectangle of the big front window. Streetlight the color of watery milk leached through the curtains. Jack could hear breathing and slow footsteps on the boards of the floor. He watched as a dark figure moved between him and the window.

Jack pointed the shotgun, holding it waist-high. He said, not too loud, "Freeze or I'll kill you."

The figure slowly broadened as the person turned. Jack tightened his squeeze on the shotgun's trigger. He said, "I've got a gun. Don't move."

There was a flash and the sharp bark of a gun. Jack went to his knees, trying to cut the target. He returned fire as he dropped, lost his balance, and fell onto his back.

He couldn't see the figure against the window anymore. But another shot came from somewhere at the end of the hall. The right side of his face was burning. Jack crabbed backwards a few feet, his bare skin squeaking against the floor, before turning over and crawling into his bedroom. The box of shells was under the bed. He groped with one hand, watching the doorway, sure that any second someone would come through it.

Jack found the shells. He loaded one into the shotgun and gripped another with his teeth. Back on his feet, he paused at the doorway and listened. All he could hear was his own breathing, his own heart pounding. He moved into the hallway, then the living room.

A slamming sound came from the kitchen. Jack whirled and nearly fired before he recognized it: the spring-hinged back door slapping shut. He started to run toward the sound. Thinking, kick open the door, lead with the gun, maybe get a look at the guy running away. Three strides into his run, he slammed his foot into a table leg. He stumbled—his big toe giving off instant high-voltage pain—and fell. When he hit the floor the gun went off. Pieces of drywall from the ceiling showered onto him.

Jack still had the extra shell between his teeth. He reloaded, limped to the back door, and kicked it open with his good foot. Outside, there was nothing to see but two t-shirts dancing in the wind.

Okay, Dean told himself, maybe the dude wasn't dead. But he got nailed, no doubt about it. Dean could have followed him when he crawled into that other room, could have finished him off there, but the guy had his own gun. Why buy trouble? The way he went down, no question he was hit bad. Dead or just wounded, it didn't matter, as long as Dean could say adios to Captain Flying Dickhead.

He reached to the floorboard below the BMW's passenger seat, picked up the .38, and blew away some imaginary smoke from the barrel. Knives, guns, whatever it takes, he thought. Dean Dudley gets the job done.

Dean drove down Mockingbird Lane. Garth Brooks on the tape deck, nobody on the road now. The sign at the old Dr Pepper plant said 4:35. Another hour or two and the sun would be up. Time to go home, Dean figured, grab a little sleep, then put the whole plan into action. Sandra didn't want to do it today? Too bad. Somebody else was in charge now. Dean Dudley was calling the shots.

He parked across two spaces at the Uptown Manor apartments and left the gun in his car. Dean was whistling as he
walked down the hall to his apartment. Feeling number-one
primo, rocket-in-his-pocket fine as he unlocked his door.

Two men were sitting on his couch.

"Fuckin-A, that you, Dino?" one of them said. "Glad you
could make it. I'm Teddy Deuce, this here is Mertts. We're your
new business partners."

# 18

*J*ack stood on the dark back steps, wearing only his underwear and holding his shotgun across his chest, looking like a hillbilly lothario's worst nightmare. Nothing moved but the laundry in the night breeze. In five minutes out there he had seen no one.

Back in the house he took the shotgun room to room, peering under beds and in closets. He inspected the shredded curtains and broken glass of the front window. There was no blood. Asking himself, how do you fire a shotgun at someone ten feet away and miss?

He used the phone in his bedroom. After seven or eight rings Sherri answered, voice thick, sounding as if her head were fogged in. Jack had to let her cough for a while. Three times he told her, "Somebody just tried to kill me," before she seemed to understand.

Sherri said, "Now who would do that?"

"Maybe it's related to what I'm doing for you, maybe it's not." His face was still hurting. He looked in the mirror and saw, under the white dusting of gypsum from the ceiling, a spray of splinters embedded in his cheek. He managed to get one out between two fingernails. "Are you listening, Sherri? What I want you to—"

"Did they hurt you, baby?"

"I'm fine." He moved to the door frame where he had been standing when the shooting started. The edge of a piece of trim had been freshly gouged about six feet up from the floor. Jack compared the splinter from his face to it: same color. "But if I had been standing two inches to the right, we wouldn't be having this conversation."

"Uh-huh. Baby, you're not making much sense. You sure you're okay?"

"I'm sure. Listen, I want you to go down and check every door and window. Make sure they're locked."

"What time is it, anyway?"

"Pay attention, now. You need to make sure your alarm system is on. I'll call the police and ask them to come by and look in on you and Sandra."

That seemed to wake her up. "Do what? The police?"

"In case the person who was after me is after you, too."

A few more coughs, then: "Uh-uh. No way. I don't want the police out here. You understand me, baby?"

"Just to check on you," Jack said. "Walk around the outside of the house, make sure everything's okay."

"No police. I don't have no use for them. Never have, never will. No way, no-how. Is Sherri coming in loud and clear on this one?"

"Who the hell are you?" Dean said.

Teddy looked at Mertts. "Another guy who don't listen."

"World's full of 'em, Deuce."

"Have a seat, Dino." Teddy motioned toward a chair. "Cleana wax outta your ears and I'll tell you again. Like I said, what, two seconds ago? We're your new business associates."

"Did Ricks send you?" Dean shut the front door and came into his apartment. "That's what it is, right? Ricks found somebody else and told them, Go on over and yank Dean Dudley's chain again."

Teddy said, "Guy just set the world record, Mertts, for going from zero to pain in the ass."

"How many times I have to tell you? I'll pay you." Dean held his hands out, palms up. "The money's gonna be here any day now, and you're the first ones that get paid. All right? Man, this gets old."

Teddy glanced around the apartment. "This dump's bad enough widdout your blood onna floor."

Dean threw up his hands. "What is it with you guys? It's in your contract you have to play the badass? All right, fine, you did that. Now, can you go tell Ricks, tell him one more time, the absolute freaking second the money hits my hands, I'll drive straight to wherever he is. I'll break the speed limit, I'll run every red light."

Teddy sniffed. "Look, I'll lay it out real plain for you, Dino, 'cause I'm beginning to see you ain't all that swift. You ready? Here it comes. I don't know from fucking Ricks. Mertts here don't know from fucking Ricks. Me and Mertts is here to help you wit your plan to snatch this, uh"—he looked at a piece of paper on the coffee table—"this Sandra. We checked it over and we seen a few things could stand some improvement."

Dean froze. His voice dropped to a near whisper. "You're crazy. I don't have any plan like that."

"Told you, Deuce." Mertts stood. "Told you he'd clam up."

"I was hoping, Mertts, we'd be able to come in here and talk sense wit this joker. And, hey, we're talking sense. He just ain't receiving it." Teddy sighed. "Dino, come have a seat onna couch, we'll go over everything, work this deal out. Beginning wit, naturally, our share udda proceeds."

Dean began to edge toward the door. Mertts circled behind him and cut him off. Dean said, "I don't know what you're talking about."

Teddy looked at his watch and rubbed his face. "Fuck, I'm tired." He sighed and pulled at his shirt. "This hot soup burn ain't doing me no favors, either. . . . Well, Dino, you leave me no choice. It's all yours, Mertts."

He watched Mertts come from behind Dean to wrap one arm around his throat, with Dean trying to make a sound but nothing coming out.

Teddy said, "Dino, this is what's known as the Mertts magic. Some guy's got, maybe, amnesia? Mertts magic cures it like you wunt fucking believe."

Dean flailed but hit nothing. "Chump's got a Sansabelt in karate," Teddy said.

Mertts pulled his arm from Dean's neck as they moved into the kitchen and gripped a handful of Dean's hair. "See how hardheaded you really are," Mertts said. He bounced Dean's face once onto the Formica counter. Dean cried out. Blood gushed from his nose.

"Or some asshole, his tongue don't work?" Teddy folded his arms, watching. "Mertts magic fixes it quick."

"Good news, Deuce, a gas cooktop." Mertts leaned toward Dean's ear and spoke as if confiding. "When you got an electric range, you gotta stand around forever while it heats up."

Mertts turned a handle with his free hand. After a second or two, a circle of blue flame flared. "See what I mean?" Mertts said. Still gripping Dean by his hair, he lifted him to his tiptoes and moved him closer to the stove. He began slowly pressing Dean's face toward the burning unit.

Dean made a sound, a warm-up for when the real pain started.

Teddy said, "Don't burn his lips off, Mertts. Hard for a guy to talk to us wit no lips."

The police arrived and told Jack a neighbor heard shots. Two cops in two cars, a man and a woman who looked to Jack like high schoolers at a costume party. He told them what happened and listened as they called in the investigators.

A crime scene tech showed up. He dusted for prints around the window the intruder had used—finishing with the announcement, "No keepers"—and dug a slug out of the bedroom wall. Sometime around sunrise a detective from Crimes Against Persons came: Arturo Ramirez, the same one working the case when Jack got stabbed.

"Man, you stay busy," Ramirez said.

"Bad week," Jack told him.

"Think it's the same one? The knife didn't work, so now he decides to use a gun?"

"Now the gun didn't work. What's next, a bomb?"

"This girl you helped out the other night . . ." Ramirez wiped his forehead with a couple fingers. "I'm trying to remember the name."

"Sandra."

"I've phoned her three or four times, can't get a call-back out of her. I even went by her house—that's some place—and left a card. Haven't heard from her. She doesn't want to talk to Art Ramirez." He reached into his shirt pocket and came back with a stick of Juicy Fruit. "You'd think she'd want to cooperate, catch whoever came after her."

"You'd think."

"Just like I think you would want to cooperate." He unwrapped the gum and folded it in his mouth. "I mean, it seems to get hairy wherever you go. . . . So what do you think? This one tonight, the same guy? Or you got other troubles?"

Jack looked at Ramirez—early thirties, short hair, burgundy suit, squat face with dark eyes that burrowed into you. "It was dark."

Ramirez gave him a long inspection, then called one of the uniforms over. They talked to each other for a minute, their backs to Jack, with Ramirez pointing toward different parts of the house. The uniform walked away and Ramirez said, "Maybe some drugs mixed up in this?"

Jack swept the room with a backhand. "Look anywhere. Any drug you find came from Eckerd's."

Ramirez made a note. Jack said, "Let's say I had a name to give you, somebody I thought did it. You go talk to him, he says he was asleep in his own bed all night, what are you gonna do then?"

"Depends on what else we turn up."

"Fine. Here's a name. Teddy N. Tunstra, just out of state prison, current address unknown." Jack spelled it for him, watched Ramirez write it down. "He's pissed at me because I helped send him down. Now he's back in town making bad-boy noises."

"You think he might be the one, huh?"

Jack touched his face where a few splinters were still embedded. "Like I said, it was dark."

Dean's face was six inches from the blue flame. He screamed something, the same word, five or six times. "The fuck's he saying?" asked Teddy.

"Beats me, Deuce." Mertts raised Dean by his hair.

Teddy said, "You tryna tell us something, Dino?"

Dean managed to nod. He coughed. Blood was still flowing from his nose. His eyes were closed. "I said all right."

"He said all right. I think that means he's—oh, man." Teddy looked at a puddle mixing with the blood on the brown-patterned kitchen linoleum. "He's wet himself, Mertts. Watch where you step, there's piss everywhere."

Mertts glanced at his new gray boots. They were lightly splattered. "It's all right, 'cause ain't nothing cleans up nicer than lizard skin."

"You say you're ready to do business wit us, Dino?" Teddy started to lean against the refrigerator, straightened to check for grime, then relaxed against it. "That what you're tryna say?"

Dean gave another nod.

"That dint take long, Mertts. Might be a record for you, man." Teddy stepped out of the kitchen and looked down the hallway. "Hey, you wanna escort Dino to the back, let him wash up, put on some clean clothes, then we can talk?"

"You got it, Deuce."

While they were gone Teddy looked over the file he and Mertts had stolen from Jack Flippo's office: Four typewritten pages detailing Jack's investigation, and his suspicion that Dean Dudley planned to hustle his rich wife by snatching Sandra Danielle. It looked like the ideal setup—a chance to make large money and settle an old score at the same time.

Five minutes, Mertts and Dean were back in the room. Dean had clean clothes on and held a handkerchief to his nose. "Think I busted his snout," Mertts said.

"Dino, have a seat." Teddy patted a place on the couch next to him. "Some things I don't understand here, but we'll get to that later. First thing I gotta ask is, how much you planning to scam wit this plan?"

"Two hun—" Dean had to stop, cough a little and clear his throat. "Two hundred thousand."

Teddy pointed to a page. "But this paper here says your old lady's got tree million."

Dean nodded and looked at the floor. "It's just that . . . I mean, two hundred thousand is . . . well, that's what I thought I could get."

"Get outta here. Tree million hanging out there and two hundred K is all you can nab? What are you running here, a discount kidnapping service? First thing we fix is the price. Right, Mertts?"

"Top of the repair list."

"Dino, you're lucky we come along." Teddy put an arm over Dean's shoulder. "This'll be the best day of your life, man, the day you met us. Right, Mertts?"

"As usual, Deuce."

# 19

"Dino, it's a good thing you decided to cooperate." Teddy drove the Jag through the morning traffic with Dean beside him. "I'm glad you seena light."

Dean dabbed at his bloody nose with a handkerchief. "You really think you can get that kinda money from Sherri?"

"Hey, it's her kid, right? If she's got it, she'll cough it up. That's what I'm thinking. That what you're thinking, Mertts?"

From the back seat, "Sounds like a winner, Deuce."

"So what we do now," Teddy said, "is you give us a tour. You show us where your old lady lives, show us where you're gonna make the snatch, then where you're gonna stash the eel bitch while you wait for the ransom."

"The what?" Dean said. "Eel bitch?"

"The one from the TV show, Sandra, unless you got somebody else you're planning to grab." Teddy gunned the Jag through a yellow light at Preston and Lovers. "Hey, Dino. Ask you a personal question. You gonna use your share udda proceeds to get a better apartment? That one you got now, I gotta tell you, ain't no way to live. I seen a roach big as my thumb onna sink."

"Hey, wait'll you see this house I should be living in." Dean nodded fast. "The house I'm supposed to own half of, on account of I'm married."

"This don't make sense," Teddy said. "You own a house, you move in."

"I did, I moved in." He nodded even faster. "I did. Right after me and Sherri got married, I walk in with my suitcase, right? I'm telling myself, look at this beautiful home, Dean Dudley, you got it made now. I wake up the next morning and she's thrown all my clothes in the swimming pool."

"Oh, man, she was lucky enough to be Mrs. Teddy Tunstra? I'd have her upside down by the ankles while she pulled every piece out wit her teeth."

Dean put the handkerchief to his nose again. "The next night, when I'm trying to sleep, she turns on every stereo, every TV in the house, top volume. I turn them all off, okay? I make it back to sleep. Two in the morning, what does she do? She turns on the burglar alarm and opens a window. So the siren goes off. Try sleeping through that."

Mertts said, "Now you're talking cold-blooded."

"The next morning she burns my breakfast black. For lunch, she says she's gonna make me a chicken sandwich, but the chicken she puts on the bread is raw. Hey, I'm not talking about not cooked enough. I mean raw."

"Whoa," Teddy said.

"I told her for supper we're going KFC."

A light changed and Teddy gassed the Jag up Preston. "So all this shit, that's how come you moved out?"

"No, man, I moved out 'cause she told me she'd give three thousand dollars a week for living someplace else."

"Tree grand a week? Just to leave?"

"Plus rent."

"So, Dino, let me ask you." Teddy looked for something he liked on the radio, with every other station playing country. "This big kidnap plan you got here. How bad did it fuck you up when your old lady goes out and hires Jack Flippo?"

"You don't have to worry about him. I took care of him."

Teddy pulled into a parking lot first chance and stopped

the car. He turned to Dean. "The fuck you talking about?"

"Last night I'm talking about." Dean made a gun with his fingers. "Boom, boom, and boom. Popped him three times—might even have been four—with my thirty-eight."

"What thirty-eight?" Mertts and Teddy said together.

"The one that's in my Beemer. Hey, you two think you're the only two guys in the world who can take care of business? Think again." Dean raised the finger-gun and blew smoke from its barrel. "Think Dean Dudley."

Teddy looked across the parking lot, then asked quietly, "Where's the body?"

"Hey, man, I don't know. Still in his house, I imagine."

"Where'd you nail him?"

"Like I just said. In his house."

"No, fuckhead." Teddy brought his eyes back to Dean. "I'm talking about where inna body."

"What—" Dean stopped, took a couple of breaths. "Look, man, he dropped like a rock. You hear what I'm saying? He went *down*. That's all I needed to see."

Teddy nodded. "Lights on when you popped him?"

"What, I'm gonna walk in his house with the lights on?" Dean tried a laugh. "Maybe ring the doorbell, say, Hi, can I come in, I'm here to blow your ass off the face of the earth?"

Teddy put the Jag in gear. "So you dint stick around to see how bad you left him?"

"Hey, what's to see? I'm telling you I shot, he dropped."

The Jag was back on Preston, cruising speed. Teddy to the mirror: "You catch all this, Mertts?"

"Amateur night," Mertts said.

Dean turned to Teddy. "What are you talking about?"

"Shut up," Teddy said. "I'm thinking."

Nobody said anything for a few miles except for Dean giving directions: Catch a left here, two lights, a right, and this is the street, Strait Lane.

Teddy made the turn onto Strait and stopped. "It's down

this street? Here's what's gonna happen. You listening, asshole?"

"Me?" Dean said.

"We're gonna cruise this street once, see the house. Then we're gonna go straight to Jack Flippo's place. You put him away? That what you're saying?"

Dean cleared his throat. "Hey, I mighta just winged him good. That's what I'm telling you. I'm saying he dropped, man. Could be he's still, you know, still breathing but hurt bad."

Teddy drove. "I wanna see it wit my own eyes."

As they approached the house Dean whispered, "Here it comes, on the left, that big white one with the round roof."

Teddy slowed. Saying, "Will you look at that."

"Yeah," Dean said, "it's like this awesome place. It's gotta be worth—oh, shit. Oh, no."

Teddy, still driving, reached with one hand and grabbed Dean's hair. "You see what I'm seeing, asshole?" He pushed Dean's head forward, nearly mashing it into the dash.

Dean said, "You gotta believe me, man, he went down. I don't understand this. He went down."

Teddy drove past the house. Saying, "Hey, chump, he mighta went down last night, but he's up now. Jack Flippo, up and walking. That's the way it looks to me, Dino. How's it look to you, Mertts?"

"Deuce, I don't even see no bandages on the boy."

"Deadeye Dino." Teddy released Dean's hair with a shove of his head. "Shoots inna dark, runs like hell. Next time somebody's after my ass? I hope it's you, man."

Dean turned and gazed out the back window. "I don't get this one bit. I mean . . . "

Teddy reached the end of Strait Lane. "Hey, it's all right. I'm happy about it, you wanna know the truth." He poked Dean in the shoulder.

Dean winced. "Yeah?"

"Yeah," Teddy said. "'Cause I still get to croak the motherfucker myself. I'd go back and do it right now, there wasn't cash money onna line."

"Gotta pick your spot," Mertts said.

Teddy gassed the Jag. "Something to live for."

It was eight in the morning by the time Jack got rid of Detective Arturo Ramirez. He bandaged the big toe he had stubbed, plucked the splinters from his cheek, and drove to the Omerdome.

Jack parked in the greystone circular driveway and stepped from the car. Beams of sunlight slanted through the live oaks. Blooming geraniums lined the sidewalk. The air had a crisp freshness to it, and a light breeze brought a scent of wisteria.

All Jack really noticed was that his head hurt and his mood was turning sour.

He thought about Howard Bell's theory of rot. He hadn't found it all yet, but this case surely had it. The smell of it was strong.

A burgundy Jaguar with heavy tint on the windows passed along Strait Lane. Jack watched it go, then walked—feeling every step, unbelievable how much a smashed toe could hurt— to the front door of the Omerdome.

Sherri met him at the door with "You poor banged-up thing."

"You do what I asked you to?" he said as he came in. "All the windows and doors secure?"

"Locked tighter than Miss Texas's knees." Sherri was walking away, toward the North Pole Room. Jack followed and took a seat on the same couch he'd been on the second day he was here.

"Where's Sandra?" he asked.

"Sleeping in. She'll be down in a while." Sherri lit a ciga- rette, blew smoke toward the dome. She was wearing cham- pagne-colored silk pajamas with the top two buttons of the shirt undone. "I asked her did she want some breakfast but she said you wore her out on the boat trip yesterday, she had to rest."

Sherri smiled and crossed her legs. "Sandra told me a little bit of it. Sounded like fun."

She leaned forward to scratch her ankle and let Jack see for free what the patrons of Louie Click's club on Commerce Street had paid hard cash to look at thirty years ago.

"Look." Jack turned away, rubbed his eyes, then faced Sherri. "Let's talk business. I wrapped things up for you. You asked me to find out who was trying to grab Sandra."

"Sure did."

"It doesn't make me happy to tell you this, although from what I've seen it won't throw you into spasms of grief."

"Uh-huh?"

"I'm certain your husband's involved."

Jack waited. Clouds of smoke went toward the dome. Sherri took the news with the hint of a smile.

"I wouldn't laugh this off. I don't know if he's after money or he's just a wacko who wants to hurt some people, but you've got a problem."

"You think that was Dean coming after you last night?"

"Could have been. Does Dean have a gun?"

"Now how should I know, baby? What I'm asking is, will he get arrested for it?"

"Not today, unless he breaks down and confesses."

"Too bad."

Jack shook his head, puzzled. "I thought you didn't want the police in on this."

"Do I want 'em coming in here and mucking around, asking a bunch of questions and telling me what to do? Acting like cops, I'm talking about. Hell, no. But when you got enough to send Dean to jail, I say, hey, let's call the law."

"Well, I don't have enough to send Dean to jail. What I do have is—"

"Then you haven't wrapped things up. I wanna know the stuff that'll put Dean away. He's the one doing this? Trying to grab my beautiful child now that I've finally put all these years of heartache behind? Then Sherri wants to see his sorry ass busting up rocks in the Texas state penitentiary."

"They don't bust rocks anymore."

"Whatever it is they do, that's where I want him." She stabbed a crystal ashtray with her cigarette butt. "Remind me later, baby, I got today's payment for you in the kitchen. Tomorrow's, too."

He waved a hand. "You don't need me now. What you need to do is to deal with Dean. I'd say start with some personal security. First, move Sandra someplace else. Better yet, send her back to California."

"I just got her back after thirty-four years. I'm not shoving her out the door now."

"Next, get a guard out here, or put a watch on Dean. Then go to court." Sherri was shaking her head, but Jack kept talking. "Find a sympathetic judge to issue a protection order. Dean'll be enjoined from coming anywhere near you. File for divorce while you're at it."

"And let some damn lawyer bleed me dry? Not in this life." She rested her head against her open hand, looking weary. "Let me tell you something. All my life, every man I've been with, it's turned bad. Every one."

Jack nodded. "I can understand that, Sherri. Believe me, I can. But I think right now you've got to—"

"You say, what about Omer Plunkett? He left the big bucks behind, didn't he?" Sherri sat up straight and faced him square on. "Tell you a little something about Omer. He used to bring his secretary home two or three days a week. Didn't matter if I was here or not, they'd go straight upstairs to that bedroom. The same bed I slept in every night, baby, smelling her perfume on the sheets and finding her hair on the pillow. You think money makes up for something like that?"

"Sherri, let's talk about right now. Let's talk about Dean."

"What about him? He's a piece of shit just like all the rest."
She sat back in her chair and looked at the ceiling. Then she
began to cry. Wet mascara trails ran down her cheeks. "One
thing you have to understand, baby. When my little girl Sandra
came home? That's the first time something's gone right for
Sherri in I mean forever."

"Tell you something, Dino. Give you a tip, all right? You're
gonna take care a somebody, you do it. Understand? No fucking
around, shooting wit your eyes closed." Teddy turned the Jag off
Strait Lane. "You just do it."

Dean cleared his throat. "I was wondering how long we'd be
out."

Teddy looked him over. "Out? Outta what?"

"I mean today. This morning. 'Cause this guy Ricks—"

"Here we go wit the Ricks again."

"—that I was talking about? See, every day I have to go by
the bar he works at and show him I haven't skipped town. 'Cause
I like owe him some money."

"You work for us now, Dino," Teddy said. "You don't got time
for other stuff. The fuck is this Ricks, anyway?"

"He's just a—you know, just someone." Dean shrugged. "I
owe him for some bets I placed."

Teddy waved at the air. "So tell him to go screw himself,
you'll pay him when you pay him."

"I don't think he'll go for that. I mean, he's a hard dude to
say no to."

Teddy glanced in the rearview mirror. "You catching any of
this, Mertts?"

"Needs a pro's touch, Deuce."

"This guy Ricks." Teddy paused at the mirror to check his
hair. Then to Dean, "This guy Ricks—is he gonna get inna way
of what we're doing?"

"Well, he kinda drops by my apartment sometimes unexpected. And he, you know, he wants his money now. So he's sorta been messing with the schedule of the whole plan."

"Let's go see him," Teddy said. "You know where to find him?"

"This time of morning? His house, I guess." Dean had been there once a year ago to make a payment. Ricks lived in a nice four-bedroom job just off White Rock Lake. If Dean got lucky he could find it again. Maybe Ricks had made it easy for him and parked his red Corvette out front.

Fifteen minutes later they were there, with Dean at the front door, ringing the bell, talking to the lady of the house. She said Ricks was out for his morning run.

Teddy took the news with a nod and cruised the neighborhood, staying close to the lake. After a couple of sweeps they saw a runner in black shorts and a white T-shirt come from under a railroad overpass and head north, the lake to his right. He was followed, about twenty feet behind, by a big, dark man on a motor scooter.

"That him?" Teddy said. "Who's that with him?"

"Ricks says he's Samoan," Dean said. "Whatever that means."

"This Ricks is so big he has muscle wittim when he jogs? Like he's what, some kinda made man? Asshole." Teddy made the curve, then slowed to keep pace. The car was about thirty feet behind.

The Samoan glanced back and waved the car around. "If you'll pull up," Dean said, "I'll tell him we want to talk. But he's gonna be pissed about doing business right now. Ricks can be a real motherfucker."

Teddy checked the mirror, then looked ahead. No cars coming or going. "Hey, there's only room for one real motherfucker onnis road."

He pulled even with the Samoan and veered right. The motorbike and the Samoan careened into a ditch.

Dean said, "What are you doing?"

Teddy floored the Jag just as Ricks stopped and turned around to look. Ricks disappeared under the front of the car. The Jag felt as if it were passing over a speed bump.

Dean looked back to see the body on the road, receding from them as they pulled away.

"You paying attention, Dino?" Teddy slapped him in the back of the head. "*That's* how you take care a somebody."

# 20

Norton Luttrall wore baggy safari shorts and a white undershirt. He sat in his 1989 Buick Roadmaster on Cole Avenue, outside the Uptown Manor apartments. Norton was dogging Dean Dudley. If Dean Dudley's silver BMW went somewhere, Norton would tail it. That was his plan.

For a while he had thought about telling Jack Flippo what he was doing, then decided against it. Tell him later. And if later Norton was not around for the telling, then the letter he'd left at home would talk for him.

Only midmorning, and the inside of the Buick was heating up already. Norton felt lightheaded and weak, and wondered if he was catching the flu. Maybe he was just getting old. Nothing wrong with that, it was what he was. You look in the mirror, Norton thought, and you accept what you see.

At least he wasn't trying to do this in August. Put him in a parked car in the August sun and he might have problems. August was when he had killed Hubbel Jolly, but that was twenty-five years ago.

Hub Jolly, the sad man with the happy name, had sold out some friends. They went to prison while Hub Jolly walked free. Free to go to his girlfriend's house every Wednesday night.

A fat man of precise habits, Hub Jolly always parked his black 1969 Lincoln Continental curbside when he went to see his sweetheart. He was there at seven sharp and out by eleven. Then he drove home, stopping each time at the same Hudson filling station for a package of Slim Jims and a six-pack of Schlitz.

Norton had watched him day and night, coming to know Hub's schedule like his own. Hub sold cartons of stolen cigarettes to small groceries and convenience stores in South Dallas. He kept the crates of hot smokes in the trunk of his car. When the trunk couldn't hold any more he put some in the back seat, covering them with an old blue chenille bedspread.

After two weeks of dogging Hub, Norton made a decision: Wednesday night at the girlfriend's looked like his best chance. The woman always kept her blinds closed, and her neighbors went to bed early. The nearest streetlight was half a block away.

The next Wednesday night was a rainy one, so the electric windows on Hub Jolly's Lincoln were all the way up when, after dark, Norton popped the lock on the passenger side, opened the door, and crawled onto the back seat floorboard. Thinking, a bomb would have been a lot easier. Wire it up, then Hub turns the key on the ignition, and so long. But Hub's old friends, the ones in prison, wanted him to get a message first.

So Norton closed the door on the Lincoln, pulled the blue chenille bedspread over himself, and waited for the radium hands of his watch to sweep toward eleven. They swept, and kept sweeping. Hub Jolly didn't show. Midnight passed, 3:00 A.M., four. The rain stopped. Norton was cramped and stiff. Hub Jolly must have been having the hump of his life.

Just after six the sun came up, its light bleeding through the bedspread. By nine the heat in the black car began to build. By ten Norton felt as if he were in an oven. By ten-thirty in the morning he was having trouble breathing.

It was almost eleven when the driver's-side front door opened. Hub Jolly climbed in behind the steering wheel, smelling of Aqua Velva. He started the car and turned the air conditioner on high. Norton sat up, reached over the seat, and drew a blade across Hub Jolly's throat. Telling Hub as he did it, "From your friends."

Thirteen hours of waiting for two second's work. Norton went home that day in August twenty-five years ago and drank six glasses of ice water first thing.

Now he blinked and stirred. He was sweating, and a fly buzzed around his face. While he was remembering Hub Jolly he had fallen asleep.

"I'm planning one big-time party, so don't try to screw me on the damn mermaids." Sherri was on the phone, at a table beneath an umbrella. Jack sat across from her, watching the sunlight sparkle on the water in the pool shaped like Texas.

"Don't ruin my little girl's wingding with your problems, Dale," she said into the phone. "I need four live girls in four mermaid costumes, all of 'em with big tits and nice smiles. Four. Count every finger but the thumb. . . . I told you—no, listen to Sherri. You ready? One to sit on the north side of the pool, where the Red River'd be, one for the Gulf Coast, one for the Rio Grande, and one out west for the Pecos. . . . Well, shit, make another one, you got one whole day. And don't forget, every one of 'em in white cowboy hats."

Sherri talked a few minutes more before pressing the disconnect button of the portable phone. "There's a shortage of fishtail costumes in Dallas," she told Jack. "So I'm supposed to be happy with just three."

"And forget the Mermaid of the Pecos?"

"Exactly what I told him." She lit a cigarette. "So let's get back to you and me. What's your plan?"

"I told you my plan. You didn't like it."

"That's right, baby. So what's your new plan?"

Jack shifted in his chair. Forty one-hundred-dollar bills made a lump in his pocket. Sandra came out of the house and walked toward them with a tray: a pot of coffee, two cups, and a Bloody

Mary. Jack watched her hips move the whole way. She set the tray on the table and said, "Here we go, second round of beverages. Did I miss anything?"

Sherri said, "You get to hear Mr. Jack give us his new plan."

"Cool." Sandra pulled her chair close to Jack and slid into it.

Jack stared at the water some more and sipped his coffee. Then to Sandra, "Just to get this straight—you believe me now when I say it's Dean?"

Sandra stretched, hands above her head. "He must be smarter than he looks." She dropped both hands to her mouth. "Sorry, Mama."

"Hey . . ." Sherri waved it off. "Ain't nothing you can say about him that'll hurt my feelings."

Sandra slipped her sunglasses on. "I'm laughing at him, 'cause he seems like such a bozo, you know? But that business about the motel room with handcuffs and stuff." She gave a shiver and turned to Jack. "You really saw this?"

"You know what?" Jack rubbed his eyes beneath his shades. "You can talk about new plans all you want. If that makes you feel any better, go right ahead."

"Boy's getting testy on us," Sherri said.

"There are still only two ways out of this. Either get rid of the temptation"—Jack gestured with an open hand toward Sandra—"or get rid of the tempted."

Sherri and Sandra stared at him. Finally Sherri said, "Do what, now?"

Sandra cleared her throat. "I think what he's telling us is that either Dean has to go, or I do."

Sherri stirred her drink with a celery stalk. "In other words, the same old horseshit. Excuse me, baby, but that's what it sounds like to me." She raised her glass and pointed with the same hand. "Let's get one thing straight, Sandra's staying right here in Dallas. My little girl's got a party to go to."

"Even if Sandra goes, Dean's still around to cook up more

schemes," Jack said. "So make him an offer. He's pulling this scam for money, isn't he? Make it easy for him, give him money—"

"*Give?* Now that's a word that sticks in Sherri's craw."

"In exchange for the cash, he has to sign divorce papers and take a hike." Jack pointed to the phone. "Call your lawyer, see what he can work out."

Sherri sighed. "Mistakes don't come for free, do they?" She gazed across the pool to a patch of lush grass where four men were putting up a white lawn tent. Another sigh. "All right, I'll ask." She punched a number on the phone, identified herself, and asked for Marvin.

Sandra leaned Jack's way. "I feel like this is all my fault."

"Not unless you made Sherri marry Dean."

"This reminds me of a movie I was in. *The X-Y-Z Factor.* You see it?"

"Missed that one."

"Aliens land in Nebraska and make some of the bacteria on Earth mutate and start chewing everybody's skin off. I was the first one to see her face get eaten. Great scene in the mirror."

Sherri said into the phone, "Well, just call him on the boat, then."

"But that's what I feel like sometimes." Sandra shook her hair. "One of those aliens. You know, I came here and had this bad effect on Dean."

"My guess is Dean went mutant long before your spaceship landed."

Sherri put the phone down with, "Marvin's on a fishing boat in the Bahamas—"

"Ooh," Sandra said. "I bet it's one of those big ones with beds in it."

"—and he won't be back till Monday."

"Okay." Jack stood and walked to the pool. The water was perfectly clear, straight to the bottom. Nothing hidden, nothing to see. Nothing like everything else.

He came back to the table. "Let's smoke Dean out, then. I'll tell him we know everything and we're going to the cops. Maybe he'll run." He watched Sherri and Sandra exchange a glance he couldn't read.

"I got a better idea," Sherri said. "Forget about Dean, we'll deal with him later." She picked up the phone again. Jack listened while she made a reservation at the Mansion. "Best hotel in Dallas," she said when she put the phone down. "There's a room for you two waiting."

"That's a great idea." Sandra jumped up. "I'll go pack." She was off to the house.

"Just keep her safe there, get her to the party tomorrow," Sherri said. "That's your job, baby. Go live like an A-rab sultan for a night."

"What about you?"

"I'll call the burglar alarm people, get a couple of security guards out here, front and back."

"Guys who couldn't get jobs as cops, sleeping in their cars?"

Sherri leaned across the table and put her hand on Jack's arm. "If Dean wanted to do something to me, he'd have done it a long time ago, don't you think?"

"You're asking what I think? I think you should leave town."

Sherri kept her hand on Jack's arm. "Listen, baby. Next week this time my little girl'll be gone, back in California. I want her to have a good time before she goes." She winked. "From what Sandra's been telling me, that's your specialty. . . . You know what? I feel like taking a dip."

She tapped his arm twice and went to the cabana to change. Jack, alone at the table, used the portable phone to pick up messages.

The only one of interest came from the legman he'd hired in California. Miles Wesley was still talking like a cartoon version of a reeferhead jazz musician between sets. Saying, "Flippo, my main, s'up? Got some sweet news for you, know what I'm saying?

Got some serious-as-a-heart-attack, solid information on this actress babe you wished me to run down."

Jack checked his watch. It was a little too early to wake up Miles Wesley in Los Angeles and expect him to be lucid. Sherri came out of the cabana wearing a one-piece suit and dove into the pool about where Abilene would be.

He heard Miles Wesley's words again: solid information. Now that, Jack thought, would be a change of pace.

# 21

"You got any Lysol, Dino?" Teddy came down the hall of Dean's apartment and into the living room. "You need to get innere and cleana batroom, soon as we finish our little chat. There's pubic hairs onna floor and filt all arounna bowl."

Dean had the stereo going, reggae music. He was dancing and making up his own lyrics. Singing, "Eighty-six, mon, that asshole Ricks . . . Get your kicks, mon, by fucking up Ricks."

"Yo, I need some quiet." Teddy moved toward the couch. Mertts was slumped on one end of it, legs stretched across the carpet, asleep. "You hear me? Turnat shit off. We got business to take care of." Then a slap to Mertts's shoulder. "Wake up. We got plans to make."

Dean had his eyes closed as he kept dancing. Still singing: "He ain't worth two dicks, mon, that piece of trash Ricks . . . He dropped like a ton of bricks . . . Oh, mon, now he's a grease spot the cat licks."

Teddy got up and shoved Dean aside to get to the stereo. He removed the disc from the CD player. Dean said, "Hey, what're you doing?" Teddy stepped to the patio door, opened it, and sent the disc sailing into the Uptown Manor courtyard.

Dean stood in the middle of the room looking like a little boy whose dog ran off. "That was a brand-new CD, man."

Teddy said, "If you don't got Lysol, Mr. Clean'll do."

"Mr. Clean'll do what?"

"First, we gotta talk." Teddy backhanded some dust off the couch cushion before sitting. "Wake up, Mertts. Dino, what you want, an engraved invitation?"

Mertts awakened and stretched. Rubbing his scar and announcing, "That was a damn good nap, Deuce."

"I'm happy for you, Mertts. Can we talk now? Everybody got their sleep and their dance number outta the way?"

Dean brought a chair from the dining table and straddled it with his arms folded on the backrest. "Any other time I'd be real pissed. About that CD? But, hey, after what you did, taking Ricks out . . . I'm not even mad about my nose getting broke. You're primo with me, man. I'm ready to do whatever you want."

"I want you to shut up until I tell you talk, that's what I want." Teddy raised an index finger. "This next question is a yes or no. That means you can nod, Dino, or shake your head. There ain't a word needs to come outta your mout. You got that?"

"Got it," Dean said.

Teddy looked at Mertts, who rose from the couch and stretched as he moved near Dean. "Here's what I wanna know," Teddy said. "Have you figured out where you plan to snatch the eel bitch?"

"See, it's not that simple," Dean said.

Teddy looked at Mertts again. Mertts cuffed Dean on the side of the face, knocking him from the chair. Dean lay on the floor, clutching his ear. Whining, "What'd you that for, man?"

"Give you one more chance, Dino." Teddy motioned toward the chair. "Have another seat. This time, answer wit your head, not your mout. You got that now?" Dean stood shakily and nodded. Teddy said, "Hey, Mertts, I think he finally learnt."

"Many things get learned, Deuce, at the upside-the-head school."

"The question." Teddy pulled gingerly at the fabric around the red blotches of burns on his neck and shoulders. "Mertts, you wunt believe how much this hurts. . . . The question, Dino. Do you know where you're gonna make your snatch?"

Dean shook his head, scared eyes on Mertts. Teddy said, "Hey, Dino, you're catching on. All right, question number two. Do you know how you're gonna make the snatch?"

Another shake of the head from Dean. Teddy said, "Chump, is there *anything* you got doped out about this?"

Dean opened his mouth but stopped before any sound came out. He pointed to his lips and raised his eyebrows.

Teddy stared. "The hell's he doing, Mertts?"

"Think he's asking permission to talk, Deuce."

"Hey, it ain't Simon Says we're playing here." Teddy rubbed his face. "Man, I'm tired . . . Dino, you need to use some words, do it."

"She's—" Dean said, and flinched. When the slap didn't come he continued. "Sandra's in it with me."

The room was silent. "Wit you," Teddy finally said. "You're telling me you and the eel bitch . . ." Teddy's mouth was hanging open, his head moving slowly from side to side.

"You got it, dude." Dean sat up, some cockiness coming back into his voice. "Me and her's partners in this deal. So she's supposed to call me when it's a good time to grab her." He sniffed and nodded. "We got it all worked out."

Teddy studied his fingernails. "Hear that, Mertts? Dino and his friend the eel bitch got it all worked out."

"Boy's full of surprises, Deuce."

"Hey." Dean shrugged, palms out. "I've been trying to tell you guys all along, Dean Dudley's on the job. I mean, the quality goes in before the name goes on."

Teddy didn't look up. "Show him how much we like surprises, Mertts."

Another blow to the side of the head knocked Dean to the floor. Teddy leaped from the couch and pressed his shoe against the side of Dean's face. "The fuck you tryna to do, holding out on me like that? Huh? What else you hiding from us, asshole? Go ahead, answer the question."

Mertts said, "Don't believe the boy can talk, Deuce, when you're standing on his teeth."

Teddy backed off. "Get him up inna chair, Mertts."

When he was upright Dean said, "That's everything." He was shaking. "Swear to God."

"What about Jack Flippo?" Teddy took a packet of Certs from his jacket pocket and popped one in his mouth. "Also known as the motherfucker I'm about to croak personally. He one of your partners, too?"

"No way, man."

"What is it you hant told me about him, Dino? Long as we're coming clean here. He in onnis deal some way?"

"No way," Dean said again. "He's just some jerk Sherri hired. That dude's in the dark, Sandra told me so herself."

"Not that much inna dark." Teddy reached to the floor and picked up the file he had stolen. "It says right here he knew enough to finger you, chump."

"He got lucky. . . . Hey, he can't go pee unless Sandra tells him to. He can't scratch his butt, he has to ask Sandra first. You know what she told me? About him?" Dean tried something close to a smile. "She's got him so whipped he follows her around like a chihuahua on a short rope."

Sandra started to undress him in the hotel elevator. She unbuckled his belt as the bellman stood next to them, humming to the music and trying not to notice. When they made it to the room Jack stood next to a marble-topped table, smelling roses in a vase while the bellman put their bags in the closet. Sandra, by the far window, began to unbutton her shirt.

The bellman seemed to be in a hurry to leave. As the door shut, Sandra dropped her shirt away. Jack took his off. Her pants went to the carpet, so did his. And the rest.

For half a minute or so they did nothing but look at each other. Finally she began to come toward him, picking up speed as she crossed the room, then leaping onto him and wrapping her legs around his hips as she whipped her arms around his neck.

Jack staggered against the table. The vase tipped over and six long-stemmed roses fell to the rug. Jack picked his way among them as he carried Sandra to the bed.

When it was over and they lay in the tangled sheets she said, "Not bad. But it would have been better if the bed had been moving."

The late afternoon sun slanted through the window. Jack was close to dozing off when Sandra raised herself on an elbow and said, "Have you ever been married?"

"Me? Two-time loser."

"I'd like to hear about it."

Jack sighed. "I'm not so sure about that."

She stroked his hand. "I don't know anything about you."

So he told her about the night Eddie Lyle showed up, his old Chevy packed to the gills. Jack was in the front yard moving the sprinklers, his wife, Sally, in the house doing who knew what, maybe working on her stony silence routine.

Eddie was muscular, swarthy, early thirties. He made his living by bringing antiquities over the border from Mexico. Smuggling may have been a better word. When the antiquities business turned slow he paid the rent by hiring on as a roofer. Jack had known him for ten years. Eddie stopped by every now and then to have a beer and talk sports.

On this night he didn't want a beer, didn't want to discuss football, didn't want to look Jack in the eye. Just came to say he was moving to Idaho. He planned to find a cabin somewhere in the mountains, see if he could pick up work in town.

"What town?" Jack said. "Whichever one's close," Eddie answered. "You're crazy," Jack said. That was when Mrs. Jack

Flippo came out the front door, struggling with three suitcases, and told her husband she was going to Idaho, too.

In the months since, Jack had asked himself almost every day why he didn't fight for her then and there. He always had the same answer. It had come to him that night as he stood under the stars, feeling as if they were the only three people on an island and two of them were about to ship out: You can't keep what's already lost.

He had watched Eddie load the suitcases into his Chevy— helped him, even. Eddie said, "Shit, don't have room for this now." Standing there holding a collapsible aluminum ladder, splattered with tar from his roofing work. He asked Jack, "Hey, man, you want it?" Jack said, "Guess so." He put it in the trunk of his car as Eddie and Sally drove off.

"And that's the story," he told Sandra, "of the night I traded my wife for a used ladder."

"She just left? Wow. Did you see it coming?"

Jack shook his head. "Saw it going, though."

"What does that mean?"

"It means I never thought it would happen. But when it happened, I saw that I'd known it all along."

Around five Sandra said, "I feel like taking a bath." She raked her fingers across Jack's leg as she got out of bed. "I think there's room for two in the tub."

"Be there in a bit," he said, watching her go. When he heard the water running he phoned Miles Wesley in Los Angeles. Four rings and Miles answered with, "What it is."

"You said you have some solid information for me," Jack reminded him.

"Solid as it comes, my main," Miles said.

"Good. In English, how about."

"Hold your monkey, man, let me get my notes and my caffe latte." With Jack thinking, This is the most irritating guy I've

157

talked to this week. "Got it now," Miles said. "All right, you wished for me to find out when and how the mother of Miss Sandra Danielle passed away. Wanted me to get heavy on the particulars."

"Right."

"Problem number one. No particulars to get heavy on. Seems you're jumping the gun."

Jack rolled from bed and moved his clothes into a pile with his foot. "What are you saying?"

"Back it up for you. I got an old address for her off some traffic court records. Owner of the place is one Harry Daniels."

"Her father."

"Hey, you must be a detective . . . Anyway, bro, that particular Harry Daniels lives down in Orange County. And he's not living alone, you catch my drift?"

Jack glanced toward the bathroom. The water was still running. "No."

"Look, man. I drove down there, okay? They got a stucco house with a palm tree in the front yard. Nobody was home but I talked to the next-door neighbor, who said she's their best friend. Harry and Ellen Daniels are alive as you or me. They just happen to be vacationing in Baja until tomorrow. But whoever told you the mom was dead was dead wrong."

Jack thought he heard Sandra singing from the bath. "You're sure?"

"Hey, that's not the big news. Catch this. I tell the neighbor I'm a producer looking for Miss Sandra Danielle, star of stage, screen, and heartbreak-of-diarrhea commercials. The best friend says, 'Oh, Harry and Ellen don't talk about her.'"

"Which means what?"

"Means that they're pissed off, man."

Jack looked out the window, watching light traffic sweep by on Turtle Creek Boulevard. He said, "Whenever you're ready, Miles."

"According to the neighbor, man, a couple of years ago the lovely Sandra talked her parents into setting up a trust. So she could help them handle their affairs in the sunset years, all that bit."

Jack put one hand to his forehead. "I feel a bad one coming."

"They made her the trustee, bro, gave her power of attorney, the whole wax job. The account had about a hundred thousand in it."

"Had?"

"Sandra and the money took off about a year ago and she hasn't come back. The mom wanted to press charges but the old man wouldn't let her. Neighbor says poor old Harry still likes to catch her on that TV show of hers, but the wife gives him holy hell, so he comes next door to watch."

Jack thanked Miles Wesley and hung up. The sound of running water had stopped. Sandra was singing. Jack followed the notes, past the marble table and the broken vase. He turned the corner and found the rose stems by the sink. They had been picked clean.

Sandra lay in the steamy tub as red petals floated around her. She was smiling at Jack. Telling him, "I'm ready for you now." Reaching for him. Asking, "But are you ready for me?"

"Ask you something, Dino." Teddy unrolled some more Certs. "How come you never just took your old lady out?"

"You mean, like, to a restaurant?"

"I'm talking about instead of cooking up this whole snatch plan. Why dint you just arrange for her to have an accident or something? Slip and fall inna swimming pool one night when nobody's around. Know what I'm saying? She croaks out and you get the house and alla money, right? No muss, no fuss."

Dean sighed. "Well, I thought about it plenty, you can lay money on that, man. I mean there was lots of nights I was ready to do it right on the spot. I'm serious. Oh, man, when she was having a big-time bitch-attack? All I was thinking was shake, rattle, and roll her ass in the grass."

Teddy turned to Mertts. "Guy can't answer one simple question, you know it?"

Dean cracked his knuckles. "But, see, I got a big problem—"

"Hey, no shit," Teddy said.

"—'cause I did some stuff a few years ago and kinda got caught. I mean, I didn't think I was doing anything wrong, 'cause this lady I knew then, she was willing to give me the cash. She *was*, man, for some bets I was making. And I'm talking about *locks*, you know? Shit like taking the Cowboys and points, right? But she had this son, what an asshole, he goes to the police and everything." Dean let out a big breath. "So I'm thinking if something, you know, happened to Sherri, some kind of accident, the cops'd be on me pretty hard. 'Cause like it says in there"—he pointed to the stolen file—"I got a record."

Teddy shrugged. "Me and Mertts got more records than Slim Whitman and Zamfir put together, Dino. It don't stop us. . . . Where'd you serve your time?"

"I got..." Dean's gaze dropped to the floor. "I got probation."

"Probation?" Teddy laughed and looked at Mertts. "Figures. He wouldna lasted tree days in prison anyway."

"He tried to join the badass army," Mertts said, "but didn't make it out of boot camp."

"Hey," Dean protested, "I was in County for three weeks. That wasn't no picnic, okay?"

"Get outta here." Teddy shook his head, disgusted. "All right, look, sit down."

"There's some tough hombres in County," Dean said. "You wouldn't believe some of the dudes they get in there. Oh, man, one night I—"

"Hey, Dino. Piece of advice? Shut the fuck up till I ask a question." Teddy exhaled through his mouth against his cupped hand to make sure the mint smell was still on his breath.

"This whole fake snatch. Who thought it up, you or her?"

"Come on, man, you ask that like you don't think I could come up with something like this. Like I said before, this is Dean Dudley you're dealing with."

Teddy glanced at Mertts, who stepped toward Dean. "All right, okay," Dean said. "Sandra came to me with the idea. She said it was an easy way to make big money."

"What I thought." Teddy nodded. "All right, let's go over this one more time. The eel bitch is gonna call you when it's time to make the fake snatch."

"You got it."

"After you two link up, you take her to this safe house you say you got—"

"Oh, man, you gotta see it." Dean smiled. "I did some good work on that place."

"—and at the safe house you take some Polaroids of her hanging inna cuffs wit chains wrapped around her. That right?"

"Absolutely."

"Then you drive over and put the Polaroids in your old lady's mailbox."

"On the money, dude."

"Next the eel bitch calls your old lady and says, Hey, I been snatched, look inna mailbox if you wanna see proof, and she screams a little like somebody's sticking her witta hot fork."

"This is where it's good to have an actress," Dean said.

Teddy stood. Dean's eyes widened. "So then what?" Teddy said. "You're gonna take the phone, disguise your voice, and tell your old lady where to bring the money? Then you and the eel bitch split the take, everybody's happy?" Teddy brushed some lint from his pants.

Dean swallowed and nodded. "I mean, yeah. . . . That'll work, won't it?"

"Like the old lady's not gonna snap to your voice." Teddy walked around the room stretching his neck. "The fuck he thinks he is, Mertts, Rich Little? Good thing you got us, Dino. We'll let Mertts handle the phone. Okay wit you, Mertts?"

"Proud to serve, Deuce."

"Since we're changing plans here." Dean cleared his throat. "You mentioned splitting the take with Sandra. I've been giving it some thought all along . . . you know . . . wondering if . . . I mean, if she could be put out of the way—"

"You mean croak her out," Teddy said, "and keep her share udda ransom for yourself."

Dean pointed at Teddy. "I like that idea, dude."

Teddy shoved the back of Dean's head. "Who gives a fuck if you like it or not. Go cleana batroom like I told you before."

When Dean was gone, Teddy said, "All right, forget him. Let's finish doping this out. . . . We got the eel bitch in cuffs at the safe house."

"Got that picture in my mind," Mertts said, "and it's a sweet one."

"Then, when you talk to the old lady onna phone, you tell her you want Jack Flippo to deliver the cash."

"I'm right with you, Deuce."

"We'll have him meet us in a parking lot or something, make sure there's no cops, then take him to the safe house." Teddy smiled. "Which is where we put Flippo and the eel bitch inna tub and take care of 'em wit Dino's gun."

Mertts patted a bulge in his waistband. "Got the baby right here."

Teddy rubbed his chin. "Here's what I ain't got figured out yet: what to do wit Dino's body? I'm thinking we put him inna trunk udda Jag at the airport on our way outta town."

"Sounds good."

"Then we call the cops wit a tip that he did the snatch, so they spend all their time looking for him." Teddy laughed. "Looking for Dino, big-time kidnapper."

# 22

The Mansion's restaurant, with coral pink stucco walls and vaulted ceilings, occupied what once was the grand house of an old man who'd had too much money. The entrance from the hotel opened onto a balcony that overlooked the foyer. You could lean against the rail, Jack found, and get a clear earful from the swells passing on the marble floor below. He heard a blonde in leather pants tell her companion, ". . . and the second Rolls was a wedding present from King Hussein of Jordan."

Now Jack and Sandra sat at a window table with a nice view of dusk draining the color from the broad lawn that rolled down to Turtle Creek Boulevard. "This is good," Jack said. "But I have no idea what I'm eating." He poked his fork into a salad that looked as if it had been picked from a well-watered vacant lot. "Is there a law against lettuce and tomatoes?"

Sandra had lobster tacos. She said they reminded her of a straight-to-video movie she had been in, *The Bermuda Triangle Caper*.

When they had plunged into the main course—braised antelope for her, pan-seared ostrich for him—Jack asked, "Why did you tell Sherri your adoptive mother was dead?"

It put the brakes to Sandra's tales of Hollywood. Her face clouded over. She set her fork down and took a sip of wine. "I wondered how long it would take for you to start checking up on me . . . Did you find my ex-husband yet?"

Jack didn't answer. "No?" she said. A toss of her hair. "I'll give you a running start. He manages an experimental theater in San Francisco. Richard DeLeon. He probably has a few bad things to say about me. He sure did in divorce court. That's where he let his imagination run wild."

"I'm just wondering what purpose it served, playing the half-orphan with Sherri. To whip up her sympathy? Make her feel as if she's all you had left?"

Sandra had both hands flat on the table, her chin pointed at him. "Here's one for your files. A couple of months ago I was in Las Vegas. At the Mirage? Guess what. I took one of their towels when I checked out . . . Let's see, what else? Did you try Sister Mary Margaret at St. Francis Academy? She can tell you about the time I cheated on a math test in fifth grade." She was talking loudly enough that people at nearby tables glanced her way. "Why didn't you tell me you were poking around in my life?"

"The situation we're in—what did you expect?"

"Situation? Jesus." Sandra looked away, then back at him. "You can really seduce with words, can't you?"

"I don't usually like my clients." Jack took a bite of his ostrich. "Something about Sherri, though, appeals to me. It's hard to feel sorry for someone with that much money, but she's had a tough life in a lot of ways."

Sandra stared at him with a look Jack remembered from witnesses he was about to corner.

"I just wouldn't want someone to take advantage of her," he said. "Like perhaps someone who would pretend to be her long-lost daughter."

She waited a few seconds, then stood and dropped her napkin on the seat of the chair. As an assistant in a white jacket hustled over to fold it, Sandra stalked away and turned the corner into the main dining room. Jack left the table, doubling back through a wait-station, coming into a small darkened banquet room off the foyer as Sandra settled onto a wing chair beneath the staircase.

There was a phone on the round table next to the chair. He watched as Sandra dialed without using a directory. Her call took less than a minute and she said little, not talking loud enough for Jack to catch the drift. What he saw of her face told him nothing; she could have been getting the time and temperature.

When she finished, she detoured upstairs to the ladies'. Jack waited until she came out, then hustled back to their table and dug into his ostrich. A minute later Sandra sat down with "Okay, you're right. That's what I told Sherri and it's not true, about my mother being dead. Congratulations, you made a big discovery. Why do you want to push it?"

"I push everything."

"Maybe that's why everything pushes back."

Jack poured more wine for her as Sandra said, "She's dead to me, okay? That's why I said it. We had a falling out, we're not speaking anymore. How's that?"

She looked out the window. Then: "I'm sure you're thinking, hey, they were good enough to adopt her, bring her up, and now she's kissing them off. Let me tell you something, it's not that simple."

"Never is," he said.

Sandra reached across the table and stroked his hand. "I don't know how to prove to you I am who I say I am. All I can do is tell you what it was like, to want to find your real mother, the one who gave you life. And then——"

Her voice broke. She sipped some water. "And then when the miracle happens and you do find her, she's the wonderful, loving person that Sherri is."

Sandra turned her face toward the lawn and began to cry. The dying light caught her tears.

With Jack thinking, That's one, now two, and here comes a third. He wanted to say, Let me know when you're up to ninety-six.

\*     \*     \*

This time she didn't try to unbuckle his belt on the elevator ride up. Two steps into their room Sandra raised a thumb and forefinger to her earlobe. "My earring." Her face showed a moment of puzzlement, then awareness. "I think I left it on the table."

"I'll go down and check for you," Jack said.

She stopped him with fingers to his chest. "I'll do it."

He moved toward the phone. "Just call the restaurant and tell them to look."

Sandra already had the door open. "Won't be a minute. Order us some champagne." She smiled and was gone.

Jack cracked the door and listened for the elevator bell. Then he took the stairs, four flights down.

She wasn't in the lobby. He couldn't find her in the restaurant. The maître d' had not seen her since they left together, and knew nothing of a lost earring.

Jack went outside, passing under the white awning. He trotted across the circular driveway and zigzagged between the cars that had been valet-parked in positions according to price.

The night breeze played over his face as he stood at the crest of the lawn. He could hear the piano from the hotel bar, playing "Till There Was You."

She was down the hill, toward the street, moving across the far end of the lawn. Her billowing white dress looked like a wisp of cloud across a dark sky. Jack started to walk to her, then began to run as a car pulled to the curb.

Sandra opened the passenger door and got in. Jack stopped running as soon as he saw it was a silver BMW.

He knew everything now.

# 23

"You're even dumber than I thought you were," Sandra said. "And that's saying something."

"What are you talking about?" Dean drove the BMW up Cedar Springs, away from the hotel. "I was right there where you told me to be—"

"Oh, please. You think *that's* what I mean?"

"—and right on time, too, on the dot. Everything's on schedule." Dean looked in the mirror and raised a thumbs-up above the dash. Then to Sandra, "You're always pissed about something. Always. I mean, what's your problem?"

"You tried to kill him, that's my problem."

"Who?"

"You telling me there've been so many, Dean, that you can't keep track?"

"You talking about the flying detective? Him? Shit. He's lucky I didn't try hard. Coulda blown his ass away, I wanted. I was just showing him what happens if he keeps screwing with me."

She put fingers to both temples. "I can't believe I'm hearing this."

"I was just giving the dude a free sample of Dean Dudley."

"I know this'll be hard for you, Dean, but I'm going to ask you to think. Think what would have happened if you'd killed

167

him. Where's our plan then, with the police crawling all over everything?"

Dean was on Oak Lawn now, headed for Stemmons. He stopped at a red light and checked the mirror again. "I got some brand-new news for you anyway. Your plan wasn't worth a shit. We got a new one." With another glance in the mirror, he pressed a button that unlocked all four doors. "We got a good one now."

She shifted in the seat to face him. "Listen to me, Dean. Don't try to go rogue on me with this. Believe me when I tell you, you don't have the mental capacity to pull it off."

Dean got a green light and punched the gas. "We'll see how smart you are in about five minutes."

"What's that supposed to mean?"

"Like I said, it means we got a new plan."

Sandra balled her right fist and swung. She hit him square on the nose.

Dean made a noise, a wail. The car swerved, bounced over a curb, and veered back into the street. Dean put his hand to his face as he steered into the parking lot of a pet grooming center and came to a stop. He cupped his hands beneath his chin and caught the blood pouring from his nostrils. Crying, "Not the nose again . . . Second time . . . Jesus Christ, this hurts."

"Now," Sandra said, "are you ready to get back on track?"

Dean began to swing at her wildly with his bloody hands. She flailed back, scratching at his eyes. They filled the car with grunts and screams as they went at each other. Neither noticed the man opening the back door and climbing in until he put his arms between them. He pushed them apart like a boxing ref.

"Yo, lovebirds, break it up," Teddy Tunstra said. "Don't croak her, Dino. We ain't taken the pictures yet."

Jack got his car from the Mansion's valet parkers—they had stuck it in the back of the lot, in Siberia with the minivans and the heaps—and drove to the Omerdome.

Sherri opened the door before he rang the bell. "Where's Sandra?" she demanded. "What's happened?"

"All good questions," Jack said. "Let me ask you one. That BMW you bought for Dean—you have an extra key for it?"

Sherri's eyes ran over his face. She looked terrified. "Listen to me," she said, and grabbed his arm. "Somebody called and said they've got Sandra—"

"That didn't take long."

"—not five minutes ago. Somebody's voice I didn't recognize. I'm watching TV, the phone rings, and some man says, We've got Sandra, and it'll cost you five hundred thousand dollars get her back."

"Half a million? Man, they're swinging for the fences."

"This man said no police or they'll kill her. He said, 'Just start pulling the money together.'" She had a grip on his arm. "What in the world's going on?"

Jack patted her hand. "Sherri, it's under control."

Sherri broke free from him. "Something's gone wrong." She sank into a chair and put her head in her hands. "It wasn't supposed to happen like this. Who is this man that's calling me?"

He touched her shoulder. "I'm sure Sandra's okay. Give me the key to the BMW and I'll check on her. It shouldn't take long. An hour, maybe."

Sherri raised her head and looked at him with red-rimmed eyes. "You know where she is?"

"Pretty sure."

"You know what's happening?"

Jack almost said it: Your little girl is stealing you blind, that's what's happening. But he held back. Telling himself, See it for yourself first. See the truth.

She gave him the car key. He said, "Have a drink, Sherri. Forget about pulling the money together. Just have a drink and wait for me to get back. We'll talk then."

\*    \*    \*

They were in the back room of the Texan Trail apartment, with Sandra cuffed at her ankles and her wrists. A red rag had been jammed into her mouth. Chains were draped across her.

Teddy had the camera. He said, "You think we oughta slap her a couple times, get a little blood going before I take these pictures? Fuck, it reeks in here. What I'm saying, Mertts—"

"Yeah, Deuce?"

"—is make it look like the bitch has been mistreated a little bit. So that Dean's old lady don't think twice about parting wit her cash."

"Sounds good to me," Mertts said.

Dean said, "Well, I'm first in line," and backhanded her across the face. She tried to scream through the rag. He laid his hand across her again. "Who's feeling so goddamn smart now?" Dean asked her. Blood had splattered her white dress. "All the time telling me how dumb I was, every day. Check it out, bitch. Who's on top this time? Huh? Bet you're sorry now. Bet you're saying, hey, that Dean's a screaming genius." He hit her once more.

Mertts stepped forward. "Anybody here's due some payback it's me. After what she did to Fredrick Mertts with them eels."

Dean turned, showing a smirk. "That's your name, Fred? Fred Mertts?"

Teddy said, "Don't do it, Mertts."

"Fred Mertts?" Dean said. "Hey, where's Ethel?"

"Don't do it, Mertts," Teddy said again, trying to hold him back.

Dean didn't notice. He turned to Sandra and did his Ricky Ricardo impression. "Lucy, you got some 'splaining to do." Another backhand across her face. "Hey, Lu—"

Mertts had Dean by the throat with one hand. He lifted and pushed, moving Dean out of the bedroom and into the front of the apartment. Saying, "Nobody jokes about my name." Dean made gagging noises and turned red, pulling at Mertts's thick wrist with tiny fingers.

Teddy said, "Mertts, now ain't the time."

"Sure it is," Mertts said. They crossed the floor of the front room, a dance with Mertts leading. He opened the door and pushed Dean onto the second-story porch, backing him against the rail—a two-by-four with flimsy wooden balustrades. It cracked and fell away.

Dean tumbled backward and into the night. Mertts teetered on the edge of the porch, windmilling his arms, about to fall, too, when Teddy grabbed him by the collar and pulled him back. "Take the stairs," Teddy said.

They walked down together. Mertts said, "Dumb sonofabitch asked for it, Deuce."

"Yeah, I know he did, Mertts. But, hey, we're inna middle of an operation here." Teddy reached the bottom of the stairs first. "Fuckin-A it's dark. Can't see a thing."

Mertts groped his way to the BMW. "I got the key. Lemme turn on the headlights, Deuce."

"Good idea. Turna lights on. Dino's probly a little shook up from the fall. We'll get him back up on his feet and—" The car lights came on. Teddy stared. "Well, maybe not."

Dean lay on his back, rag-doll limp across the low rock and concrete wall, not moving. He gazed emptily, straight up, and a trickle of blood ran from his mouth. Shallow breaths came unevenly.

Teddy reached into his jacket for some latex gloves and pulled them on. Mertts walked up. "Dude shoulda kept his mouth shut in the first place, Deuce. He dead?"

"No, but he's probly wishing he was." Teddy glanced toward the BMW's headlights. "What are we doing, a stage show here? Turna lights off and let's get ridda this asshole."

Mertts killed the lights and came walking back in Teddy's direction with "Man, it's dark in this place. Ain't gonna be easy getting him back upstairs when you can't see a damn thing."

"Haul another chump up a buncha stairs?" Teddy said. "Fuck, Mertts, we gonna have this argument again?"

\*     \*     \*

Norton Luttrall sat in the dark and listened to the noise coming from the next apartment. The room was warm, the air stale. He heard the scuffle and the breaking of the railing along the second-floor porch. Norton peeped through the curtains to see two of the men walk toward the stairs. He thought: *Now*.

He had waited in his car all day. He had tailed the BMW. He had crept upstairs into this room. It was the absolute right time for him to make his move.

Norton felt all his years of sorrow purifying into this moment.

He picked up his .32 revolver and a plastic squeeze bottle full of kerosene, and stepped toward the double door that separated the two apartments. His plan: Open the doors, grab the girl, start a fire for diversion, and get out.

But his legs weren't working the way they should be. He suddenly felt as if he were shin-deep in wet concrete. Sweat poured off him, and there didn't seem to be enough air.

His hands were shaking so badly he couldn't keep one of them on the doorknob. All his capers over the years, he'd never had the shakes. His strength was draining from him like water out of a bathtub.

The dark seemed to be swallowing him. He passed out.

# 24

$\mathscr{J}$ack's idea was a simple one. He would creep up on the Texan Trail apartment, see if Sandra and Dean were inside, then disable the BMW so they couldn't make an easy exit. Give his report to Sherri and let her decide if she wanted to call the cops in. His work would be done. Jack could walk away feeling once more like someone who burned down houses to get rid of the rats.

He ran the scheme through his head as he drove down Fort Worth Avenue. Thinking that a peep into the front window of the apartment might be risky. Wondering if there could be a better way. Then remembering the collapsible aluminum ladder, from the night his second ex-wife walked out, still in his trunk.

Jack drove past the Texan Trail Motor Lodge, taking a right on the next street, going uphill a few blocks, and making another right into a tattered warehouse district short on streetlights. He cruised about a hundred yards and pulled to the side of the road. If his sense of direction was holding, the Texan apartments were across the dark field to his right. He took a flashlight from his glove box and the ladder from his trunk, and plowed into the weeds.

Junk cars and abandoned appliances loomed like boulders. The footing was muddy and uneven. Jack fell once, his right leg dropping into a knee-deep hole. He twisted as he went down, and the end of the ladder caught the side of an old washing machine. It sounded like the dime store version of a Chinese gong.

He sat on the ground for several minutes, not moving, listening for any response from the Texan: a spotlight shining his way, maybe, or dumbass Dean yelling, "Who is it?" But there was nothing.

Jack made the rest of the trek without incident. He laid the ladder under a back window and felt his way around the side of the building to the front. Upstairs, light leaked around the closed curtains of one window. Jack stepped over the low rock wall and moved toward the BMW.

Asking himself, how much damage to do? He wanted to keep Dean and Sandra in one place while he reported to Sherri. But he didn't want to tip them off that he had been there.

Jack checked the driver's-side door. It was unlocked, the alarm off. He decided to deflate one tire and let the air out of the spare, too—just the kind of situation a numbnut like Dean might naturally find himself in. First the spare, he thought, moving to the trunk.

When he opened the lid he saw Dean Dudley, face up.

Blood trailed from Dean's nose and mouth, and matted one side of his head. He drew raspy breaths. Jack said, "What happened to you?" Dean's eyes fluttered and he made a gurgling sound.

Jack pulled Dean into a sitting position to keep him from choking on his own blood. Dean coughed, then managed to say, "Fucked me up bad, man."

"Who did?"

"Motherfuckers, man."

"Which ones?"

"Fucked me up, man."

Jack helped him out of the trunk. The move to the front of the car—with Dean barely able to walk, an arm over Jack's shoulder, legs giving way every couple of steps—was a slow one. Jack dumped him into the back seat.

"Keep yourself upright," Jack said. He leaned across to put the key in the ignition. "I'll be right back, drive you to the hospital."

"Fucked me up bad, man."

Even when he was half dead, Dean wouldn't shut up. Jack closed the door quietly. So much, he thought, for having it all figured out.

"What do you make, Deuce? A real diamond?" Mertts picked up Dean's ring from the coffee table and examined it with one eye closed. "Might be worth something."

"Go to the pros, Mertts. Take it to a pawnshop." Teddy sat at a Formica and chrome dinette set, studying the Polaroids of Sandra. "You see this one? See how pissed off she looks? Looks like she's—man, it stinks innis place. Tell me why Dino hadda pick a safe house that reeks."

"Got a better one for you, Deuce." Mertts waved Dean's wallet. "Why's a dude whose old lady's worth millions only have ten bucks on him?"

Teddy sniffed his sleeve. "I'm gonna hafta burn these clothes I'm wearing, we get outta here. This smell ain't never coming out, you know it? Unbelievable."

Mertts slipped Dean's watch on his wrist and admired it. "Nice Rolex, though."

"All right, here's what I think we do. After midnight let's go pop a couple these"—Teddy held the photos up like a hand of cards—"inna mailbox at the old bag's house. Then we call her up again. Say, take a gander udda pictures, lady, you wanna see we mean business. Tell her to go get her cash from the bank first thing inna morning, and we'll be calling her to say where to send her boy Jack Flippo wit the money."

Mertts rubbed his scar. "Take the pitchers to her after midnight, Deuce?"

"So nobody spots us making the drop."

Doug J. Swanson

"That gives me time for a nap."

Teddy glanced around the room. "Only place inna world that don't have a TV, this shithole. Even prison had a TV, Mertts. . . . Man, it stinks in here. I gotta get some air."

Jack extended the ladder and raised it upright. It reached the rear window of the second-floor Texan Trail apartment. He climbed with the flashlight in his right hand, telling himself he would take a peek through the window, that's all—just to find out what's what—then drive Dean to Parkland and get on the phone to the police.

At the top the curtains were parted, the room dark. Jack peered through the dirty window, playing the frayed flashlight beam over the cartoon faces on the walls. He swept the light past a hole someone had punched in a closet door, over the dirty floor and across the bare ticking of a double bed, to a sheet of plywood on the mattress. Sandra's foot was the first he saw of her.

Next came a gleam from the shackle on her ankle. Jack moved the beam up and across her white dress, its front spattered with blood. Her face was battered and bloody, and a gag filled her mouth. She lay on her back on the plywood, pinned in a spread-eagle by four handcuffs.

Jack couldn't tell if she was dead or alive. He had to go in.

The old window wouldn't raise easily. Jack pushed as hard as he could, finally breaking the seal of grime and old paint. It went halfway up and jammed there.

Enough room for him to slither through. Jack climbed inside and got to his feet. The bedroom door was ajar. He looked through the crack and saw someone lying on a couch in the front of the apartment. He couldn't see a face, but he could hear snoring.

Then to Sandra. Jack said, "It's me," and put his hand on her cheek. At his touch she bucked and thrashed, yanking at the cuffs. The metal banged against the plywood. She tried to scream

176

through the gag. Jack climbed on her and pinned her arms and legs with his. Fear came off her like heat from a radiator.

He whispered, "It's okay . . . it's me . . . quiet . . . you're all right." Saying it ten or fifteen times until the fight finally left her.

His lips were next to her ear. "It's me, all right? It's me. Do you understand?"

She nodded. He took the gag from her mouth, ready to stuff it back in if she started to scream again. Jack put a finger to her lips. "I'm going to get off you now. We'll get out of here together. All right?" She nodded again.

"Who's out front?"

"It's those two," she whispered. "With a gun. *Those* two." She said it as if he were supposed to know.

He didn't have time to figure it out. "Get you off this board first," he said.

Each manacle was half a pair of handcuffs, with the short bits of chain nailed to the plywood. Jack remembered Dean's tools from his first visit to the apartment. He scoured the room with his light and found the open toolbox in one corner.

A pair of twelve-inch bolt cutters with red handles lay beside it. Jack used the cutters to sever the chain of each shackle, starting with the ankles and moving to the wrists. "Can you walk?" he whispered.

She nodded. "I think so."

Jack helped her up and moved her to the back wall. Saying quietly, "The first step'll be the tough one." He stuck his arm out of the window and felt for the top rung of the ladder. All he got was wall and air. He put his face through the opening and looked. The ladder was gone.

Light swept the room. Jack pulled back from the window and turned to see Teddy in the doorway, pointing a gun.

Teddy was smiling. He said, "What you gonna do, Jackie, fly outta here like a fairy?"

# 25

Mertts hammered horseshoe-shaped nails to secure Sandra's cuffs to the plywood. The gag had been stuffed back in her mouth. She lay on her back and locked eyes with Jack, blinking only when the hammer hit. She had the look of someone who could hear the gears of the machinery lowering her casket into the ground.

"I mean, it was like a present, you showing up," Teddy said. He had his gun to the back of Jack's head. "Like Santy Claus." He pushed the gun hard against Jack's scalp. "Let's go up front."

They moved out of the bedroom and into the front of the apartment. "Onna couch," Teddy said. Jack sat, with Teddy standing behind him, the gun pressed against the top of Jack's head. Teddy said, "Hey, Jackie, check it out: I put a bullet in you now, it'll go through your brain and right out your ass."

Mertts came in, rubbing his head, heaving a sigh. "Man, I need another pill. The noise from that hammering . . . "

Teddy leaned close to Jack. "Mertts is pissed 'cause his nap got interrupted. So he ain't too happy wit you, Jackie. I'm telling you this as a pal, 'cause I know you make a lotta wiseass remarks. I wunt do that right now."

Jack watched Mertts go to the kitchen sink and splash water on his huge face, running his hand over the zipper scar and the golden ringlets of hair. He moved slowly but with power, like a big bear trying to wake up.

Mertts dried his face and said, "Now what was you telling me about Christmas?

"It was unbelievable, Mertts. I step outside to get some fresh air, right? I'm just standing downstairs by the wall, I hear a noise around back. I'm going, the fuck was that?"

Teddy lowered the gun to Jack's neck just below the hairline. "I walk around back to check it out, and what do I find? A ladder. I look to the top udda ladder and what do I see? I see somebody climbing inna window."

Mertts smiled in wonder and shook his head. "Strange things just keep on happening in this life, don't they, Deuce?"

"Then, bah-da-bing, bah-da-boom, I take the ladder down, I run back inna house, I open the door to the bedroom, and it's my pal Jackie, come for a visit . . . C'mere, Mertts, and take over for a minute."

Mertts moved behind the couch. Jack felt a slight jostling of the gun barrel against him. Then Teddy stood in front, saying, "Guy I been chasing from here to East Jesus, Mertts."

"Like going fishing," Mertts said, "and having one jump right into the boat."

Teddy walked to the bedroom. Mertts, still behind Jack, kept talking. "I seen that happen once. Gulf of Mexico, big old sailfish made a jump, landed right in my buddy's boat. You think I'm lying?" He nudged the back of Jack's head with the gun barrel. "Huh? You think that?" He pushed harder.

"No."

"Go check my buddy's wall. Two-car garage he converted to a den? That fish hangs over his wet bar to this day, I shit you not."

Teddy was back in the room, carrying the twelve-inch bolt cutters. He got a chair from the dinette set and sat in front of Jack, knee to knee. "So you did me a favor, Jackie, coming inna window like that."

"In return," Jack said, "I want you to let Sandra go."

Teddy laughed. "Hey, Mertts, he wants me to let the bitch go. You believe that?"

"Put a gun to somebody's head, Deuce, they start thinking some weird shit."

"He's thinks he's a funnyman."

"You've got me," Jack said. "You've made your call to her mother. You don't need Sandra anymore. Set her free."

"My question to you, Jackie?" Teddy leaned his way. "You're so fucking smart, how come you're the one onna couch wit a gun pointed at that peanut you call a brain?"

Jack said, "She's no use to you—" He stopped when Teddy brought the bolt cutters to his mouth, the cold blades touching his lips. Jack smelled the oily steel mixed with the scent of Teddy's breath mints.

"I'm so fucking tired of hearing you, Jackie." Teddy moved the blades around the outside of Jack's mouth. "My ears start to hurt every time I hear your weaselly little voice, you know it? Hey, I'm asking you a question."

Mertts prodded the back of his head with the gun barrel. "He's asking you a question."

Jack swallowed hard. "Whatever you say, Teddy."

"Here's what I say, asshole." Teddy brushed the blades against Jack's cheek. "I say you're a lucky fucking guy. Only reason I hant flushed you downa toilet already is you're gonna be my bagman, Jackie. You're gonna be the one the old lady gives the money to. Me and you, we'll go to her house inna morning. You'll tell her to hand over the cash. I'm thinking she sees you, she won't try to pull no shit. And maybe if you cooperate I won't hurt your girl-friend. Your little piece of chained heat innere . . . Ever catch that movie, Mertts? *Chained Heat?*"

"Missed that one, Deuce."

"Fucking classic, man. I seen it six times . . . Inna meantime, Jackie"—Teddy ran his tongue over his teeth—"I'm thinking I give you a little sample of what happens if you get stupid and try to screw wit Teddy Deuce when we go to pick up the cash."

The blades were at Jack's nose now. Teddy said, "How about a nose for a nose. You think I forgot what you did to me wit the pliers, Jackie? Anyway, you could stand to lose a little here. I snip an inch or two off, I'd be doing you a favor . . . What do you think, Mertts? A finger? A toe?" Teddy moved the blades down and pressed them against Jack's crotch. He smiled. "A cock?"

"All excellent choices," Mertts said.

"So how do I pick what I'm gonna cut, Jackie? Eeny-meeny-miney-moe? Catch an asshole by the toe? Or do I close my eyes and point to a spot? You tell me, Jackie. Tell me how I'm gonna—" Teddy stopped, raised his head, and sniffed. "The hell is that smell?"

Norton Luttrall was finally able to stand. How long he could stay upright, he didn't know.

In the dark he couldn't find his gun. He had crawled around the couch, feeling for it on the floor and between the cushions, and found nothing. Norton was left with only one weapon, but it was his favorite.

With his right hand he gripped a quart jar of kerosene. In his left hand was an old plastic squeeze bottle that once held ketchup. Now it, too, was full of kerosene. He bent and dropped the plastic bottle to the linoleum floor. Using his foot, he moved it to the double doors that connected to the next apartment.

Norton listened to the angry voices coming through the walls. He recognized Jack's, and heard enough to figure out Jack wasn't in charge.

The spout of the bottle poked into the gap between the underside of the doors and the floor. Norton placed his shoe on the bottle and pressed. He felt it flatten as the kerosene flowed out. The smell of it brought back memories of an overinsured two-story house off Lemmon Avenue, of a failing insurance agency on Elm Street, of a bar on Northwest Highway whose owner had pissed off the wrong people.

All had been torched by a much younger Norton Luttrall. Each fire had, in its own way, been a thing of beauty. They were surgical jobs—fast burners, with no adjacent structures damaged. Nobody hurt, nobody convicted. He remembered how it felt putting match to fuel: the sudden sound of combustion, the pure smell of hot vapors, the quick dance of flames across the floor and up the wall.

Now, with the plastic bottle empty of kerosene, Norton reached for the doors separating the two apartments. His hands were unsteady and his balance unsure. He had to lean against the knob for a few seconds. A wave of nausea washed over him. Norton pulled the first door open. He pushed on the second. It was stuck. He pushed harder—feeling as if he had used his last particle of strength—and the door swung free.

He saw three people: Jack on the couch. A large man behind him with a gun. Another one, his back to Norton, in a chair.

The one in the chair stood and turned. He looked at Norton and said, "The fuck is this?"

Norton plunged his free hand into his pocket and pulled out a match. With a flick of his thumbnail, the match was lit.

# 26

Jack had looked past Teddy's shoulder to see the liquid spreading across the hard, shiny floor. Fumes crawled up his nose. He thought something had sprung a leak. Thought it until he saw Norton Luttrall.

The door had opened and there he was, like a surprise guest on the old *Dean Martin Show*. The first question in Jack's mind: Whose side is he on?

Teddy said, "The fuck is this?" And from behind Jack, Mertts with "Who in hell is that, Deuce?"

Norton had lit the match with his thumbnail. Then he started to talk, had to clear his throat, and started again. Looking at Teddy but gesturing with the match toward Jack. Saying, "Let him go and the girl, too. Or I burn this rat trap to the ground with you in it." His voice came in weak and spotty, like a radio station out of range.

Teddy laughed as he rose from the chair and stepped toward him. He stopped at the edge of the liquid. "You're gonna do what?" The thin lake of fuel separated them by four or five feet. It slowly broadened on the sloping floor, and the smell of it filled the room. Teddy glanced back. "The fuck did this guy come from, Mertts? The planet of old men?"

Norton's fading voice: "You got about ten seconds."

Teddy stood on his toes and craned his neck, looking into

183

the next apartment. "Anybody else innere wit you? No? Tell you what Teddy Deuce'll do for you. I'm gonna give you one chance to blow out the match and go back to your nursing home. Do yourself a favor, gramps, and go chase some granny pelt."

The match in Norton's left hand had burned down past halfway. Norton said, "Put the gun down and walk out. Right now." Jack felt the barrel stay cold against his neck. Norton swayed, and his knees looked as if they were about to buckle. His mouth was going slack.

"Watch this, Mertts." Teddy, still on the dry part of the floor, leaned toward Norton and blew like the wolf outside the pig's house. The match flickered but didn't go out. "Well, shit," Teddy said without looking back at Mertts. "Go ahead and do him."

The barrel left Jack's neck. He looked up and to his right to see Mertts pointing it at Norton. Jack lunged for the gun.

He got one hand around the cylinder, squeezing it. If it couldn't move, Mertts couldn't fire. Jack's other hand gripped Mertts's huge wrist.

Teddy still had his back to them. He shouted, "Mertts, *do* the motherfucker."

Joe Gentile had tried to shoot him in 1959, at a dance club out on Harry Hines Boulevard. A short bald guy with thick glasses, Joe Gentile. He looked like Mister Magoo at target practice. The first shot had gone wild, and Norton hadn't hung around for the second. Even dumps on Harry Hines had back doors.

Now somebody else was pointing a gun at him. This time Norton had no reason to duck and run. All he wanted now was the strength for one last act.

Norton saw the gun in the hands of the big man. He heard the one who called himself Teddy Deuce shouting, "Do it."

He raised the quart jar of kerosene to shoulder height and used everything he had left to throw it at the feet of Teddy Deuce. As the glass shattered he tossed the match.

There was a sudden wave of heat. Norton was falling backward. The last thing he saw: flames licking their way up the legs of Teddy Deuce.

Mertts punched him twice in the head. Jack lost his grip on the gun with the second blow. Hot billowing air washed over him, and someone fell against the couch.

It was Teddy, on fire from the knees down, a high staccato wail coming from him. As he batted at his lap, his sleeves caught fire.

Jack rolled off the couch and away from the blue and yellow flames rising off the floor. He was still woozy from the punches. Teddy was up, spinning crazily, slapping at the flames as they spread over the sleeves of his jacket. He pinballed off two walls, then staggered out the front door, screaming.

The bolt cutters lay on the floor next to Jack. He gripped them as Mertts stepped past him. Jack got to his knees.

Mertts moved toward the doorway that opened into the next apartment, as close as he could get without stepping into the flames. He raised the gun and fired once. The fog cleared enough in Jack's head for him to understand that Mertts was shooting at Norton.

Jack struggled to his feet, behind Mertts. Mertts steadied the gun to fire again. Jack swung the bolt cutters and caught him in the side of the head. Mertts dropped to the floor as if his power had been cut.

The gun lay next to him. Jack scooped it up and stuck it into his waistband. The room was beginning to smoke up. An upholstered chair had caught, and Jack saw that the fire would spread to some curtains next. He picked up the bolt cutters, stepped over Mertts, and ran to Sandra in the back room.

Her eyes were wild with fear. He said, "We're getting out of here." Jack snipped the horseshoe nails that held the wrist cuffs. Sandra pulled her gag out as he freed her ankles. She burst from the plywood and tried to go for the window. He wrapped his arms around her waist.

Talking to her, his mouth at her ear: "You're all right. You're okay. We're getting out now. You're with me. Let's go." Smoke had begun to float into the room along the ceiling. He could hear the growing sound of the fire. Jack turned Sandra around, pointing her toward the door, and she screamed.

Mertts stood in the doorway, filling it up. Blood oozed from the gash on the side of his head, as if the zipper scar were leaking. In his hands was a leather belt, its end running through the buckle to form a noose. Mertts was smiling. He said, "Can't hurt a steel plate."

Jack pulled the .38 and fired. The big man clutched his throat as he fell.

# 27

They were coughing as they reached the bottom of the stairs. Jack led Sandra to the low rock wall and let her sit, giving her a few seconds to suck in some clean air. The cuffs still hung on her ankles and wrists like odd jewelry. He pointed downhill to the motel office. Get down there as fast as you can, he said, and call the fire department. Tell them to send an ambulance. Better yet, send two.

Then Jack ran back upstairs to find Norton.

Apartment 4 was ablaze, with the windows full of fire like wide, demonic eyes. Jack kicked open the door to number 3. He peeled off his shirt, tied it over his face in a bandit's mask, and crawled in.

He had never known that fire could be so loud. It seemed to swallow his calls for Norton. A surge of billowing smoke rolled across the room. Jack dropped flat on his belly, and could barely see beyond his hands. His eyes and lungs burned.

Just when he thought he could go no farther, his hand touched Norton's shoe. Norton was on his back, not moving. Jack clasped each of his ankles and crawled backward, pulling Norton as he went.

The door was not where he thought it would be. He let go of Norton and felt for it, finding only wall. The heat seemed to spike, making the bare skin of his trunk and arms feel as if it

187

would start to bubble. He was coughing hard, and thought he was about to pass out from the smoke.

Jack ran his hands along the baseboard: still nothing but wall. He raised up on his knees and groped blindly for the window. Fear had him. He dropped onto his side and kicked at the plasterboard in a panic. One kick struck only air. He had found the doorway. Jack backed out, pulling Norton as he went.

He jackknifed Norton over his shoulder and staggered along the porch to the stairs, wondering how a little man could be so hard to carry, as if old secrets and past sins weighed him down like lead in his pockets.

Jack's legs were rubbery as he reached the bottom of the stairs. He carried Norton across the dirt parking area and set him down under a cottonwood tree.

Both of them were hacking away, a good sign: Coughing meant Norton was alive. Jack cradled the old man's head in one arm. Norton's eyes fluttered open, then dropped shut again. "You'll be all right," Jack told him. "Help's on the way."

Norton rasped something between coughs. Jack bent to hear the old man asking, "Did the girl get out?"

"Sandra made it fine," Jack said. "So will you, soon as that ambulance gets here."

He gazed down the hill. Thinking, the sirens should be wailing by now. There had been plenty of time for Sandra to run down and make the call. Norton groaned. Jack figured he would give the ambulance another minute or so. If it didn't come, he would put Norton in the back seat of the BMW and drive him and Dean to the hospital together.

The car was across the dirt lot, about fifty yards away. Easier to bring the BMW to Norton than carry Norton to the BMW. Jack got up and trotted toward it, skirting the low rock wall.

The roof of the building was in flames now. Jack thought about the body of Mertts still inside. He had seen men killed before, had caused them to be killed, had wanted to kill some of them. But until tonight he had never done it himself.

Jack felt the gun in his back waistband, dead metal against his skin. He pulled it out, studying it as he ran. The blue steel glimmered in the firelight. He thought about how he had shot, and how Mertts fell.

What surprised him now was how easy it had been. That, and the feeling he could do it again if he had to. Jack had not a drop of remorse in him.

He had sat across the courtroom from stone killers for years, had been paid by Dallas County to make a dedicated effort to send each one of them to prison or Death Row. He had stared at them, questioned them, tried to see inside them, wondered what was in their heads. Only now did he understand the cold emptiness of their minds. He had joined the brotherhood.

Jack heard heavy footsteps behind him. As he turned to look, a blow struck him across the side of his neck. The gun left his hand as if it had grown wings. He fell, hit the stone wall, and tumbled over it.

Jack lay face down in the dirt. He wasn't sure if he'd lost consciousness, didn't know how long he'd been there. He could feel the heat from the fire on his bare back. And he heard a voice, but could make out only some of the words: ". . . always the fucking smart guy . . . "

He shook his head, trying to clear it. The voice said, ". . . but now it's just down to me and you, asshole."

Jack turned over and found himself staring up at someone standing on the other side of the low wall: a figure in the ghostly firelight who looked like one of those survivors of explosions he sometimes saw on the network news.

Teddy Tunstra said, "Where you going in such a hurry, motherfucker?"

In one hand Teddy held the gun Jack had dropped. In the other, a length of two-by-four. His clothes were tattered and scorched. Half his face had been burned black, and part of his hair had been singed away. He was covered with dirt and bits of grass and leaves.

Teddy swayed, and every breath was a groan. Jack could smell burned flesh. "Look what you fucking did to me now," Teddy said.

Jack managed to sit up. "You need a doctor."

"You know how much this hurts, Jackie?" He dropped the two-by-four but kept the gun pointed at Jack. "It hurts like nothing you ever felt before, man. But you know what?"

Teddy stumbled forward and braced himself against the wall. "When I was rolling around onna ground to put myself out? Know what I was thinking, man?"

Jack stared into Teddy's eyes and saw the same look he had imagined in his own when he shot Mertts.

Teddy said, "I was thinking, first I get Jackie, and then the little old man that set me on fire inna first place. Payback, Jackie. Nothing sweeter than that."

Jack raised up on his knees. "Let me get you to a hospital."

"I like that, you on your knees. You gonna beg now?"

There was movement behind Teddy. Jack saw the BMW, its lights off, coming toward them.

"Go ahead, Jackie, let me hear you beg. I wanna hear you cry. I wanna hear you ask Teddy Deuce to pretty please let you keep your life, which ain't worth a flying fuck."

The car was about fifty feet away, rolling not much faster than a man could walk. Jack stood. Saying, "Put the gun down, Teddy, and let's get you some help."

Teddy thumbed the hammer back and pointed the barrel at Jack's face. "Beg for it. Everything you got."

The car kept coming. Jack knew where now. He could have said something. One word, all it would have taken.

Teddy said, "Go ahead, Jackie. Tell me why I shunt feel real good about plugging you right inna face wit—"

At twenty feet away, there was a roar from the BMW's

engine and a burst of speed. Teddy whirled, saw the car, and tried to jump out of the way.

He couldn't. Because Jack Flippo, standing on the other side of the wall, had two hands on the back of Teddy's collar.

Glass, plastic, and metal crunched against rock. The bumper pinned one of Teddy's knees to the wall. Teddy fell against the hood and writhed like a worm freshly stuck on a fishhook. Jack had never heard anyone scream that loud.

Then the screaming stopped, replaced by a torqued guttural through clenched teeth as Teddy raised up. Jack lurched over the wall for him but fell short. Teddy pointed the gun toward the driver and fired. A spiderweb crack bloomed instantly on the windshield.

Teddy got off another shot, and it shattered the glass into pebbles. Jack slammed Teddy's wrist against the hood and took the gun. Teddy pleaded, "Help me, man. Oh, shit, help me, please." Then he began to scream again.

The driver of the BMW was slumped against the steering wheel. Jack opened the door and lifted Dean Dudley's head. There was a bullet hole over one eye.

He reached across the body and popped the car in reverse. When it had rolled a few feet from the wall, Jack turned the key and killed the engine.

He backed out of the car and raised his head. Over Teddy's cries, he could finally hear sirens.

# 28

Jack sat on his couch, looking out the window and thinking about the dean of the barstool law school.

It was early afternoon, with the sun shining and birds singing. What was left of Mertts lay on a stainless-steel slab at the county morgue. Same with Dean. Teddy was headed for jail if he ever got out of the hospital. Just an hour earlier Sherri had called Jack to say she was so grateful for his saving the life of her little girl that she was throwing in a bonus. Come by and get it, she told him, at the party tonight.

Now he asked himself: Why not let it end right there, with everybody dead or happy? But he kept hearing the Winston-and-whiskey voice of Howard Bell, lecturing on truth and rot. Always peel away that last layer, Howard Bell would say. Never stop until you reach the absolute core.

Jack stood and walked to his kitchen. Every small movement hurt. He had pain from head to toe.

On a scrap of paper next to the phone was a number given to him by Miles Wesley, his West Coast gumshoe. Jack read it and dialed.

Harry Daniels answered on the third ring. Jack identified himself, apologized for interrupting, said he hoped Harry and his wife enjoyed themselves down in Baja. Asked Harry if he could talk a little bit about his daughter Sandra.

Silence on the line. Then Harry said he was pretty busy, and what was this all about, anyway?

A routine investigation, Jack said. Could Harry just tell him one thing? Could Harry tell him if Sherri LeBonne of Dallas—Sherri Plunkett now, Jack said—was really Sandra's mother?

Harry said, Do what? Who?

Maybe, Jack allowed, they didn't give you that information when you adopted Sandra.

And Harry said, Adopted? Sandra wasn't adopted. Sandra, he said, was born right here in California to Ellen and me.

Hospital visiting hours started at 6:00 P.M. Norton was in a semi-private room, but the next bed was empty. Jack sat on it and said, "How you feeling, my friend?"

"Like a damn pincushion. They sent out for extra needles, just to stick in me." Norton had an IV feed, and a monitor tracked his heartbeat. A clear plastic oxygen tent encased him from the chest up. He was even paler than before, and his blue hospital gown lay on his bony body like a dust-cover drape over a Shaker chair.

"Saw the doctor outside," Jack said. "He said you're doing pretty well for an old coot who got shot in the thigh and breathed in a roomful of smoke."

Norton gave a weak backhand wave. "He looks like a kid, not a doctor. He's barely shaving." Norton sounded thin and distant through the plastic, like a voice from another room.

Jack gazed up at the TV bolted to the wall. The Channel 8 news was on, Chip Moody talking: "Two men died last night and two others were seriously injured when an apparent kidnapping scheme went awry." There was videotape of the fire department pouring water on the Texan Trail apartments, with orange flames against a black sky.

"Will you look at those colors," Norton said.

At the commercial, Jack leaned over to the TV remote control clipped to Norton's sheet. He muted the volume and asked, "A Detective Ramirez come by to see you yet?"

Norton gave another weak wave. "Couple plainclothes was here this afternoon. I told 'em I was too sick to talk, had the nurse run 'em off."

"I talked with Ramirez this morning. He said both our cases will go to the grand jury, but I don't think we have anything to worry about. I'd say a no-bill is just about assured."

"Whatever."

The door to the room was open partway. Jack got up, closed it, and pulled a chair close to Norton's bed.

Norton peered at him through the vinyl tent. "You got a look on your face, bub, like it's come-to-Jesus time."

Jack leaned forward, elbows on knees and hands folded. "Why'd you do it, Norton?"

"Do what?"

"Come on."

Norton stared toward the top of his tent, then rolled sunken eyes Jack's way. A bony shrug poked the gown. "I owed you one. From way back, when you kept me out of prison." He looked away. "That, and I felt bad about getting you in this whole mess in the first place."

Jack shook his head. "Run that last one by me again."

"She called me one day three or four weeks ago. Sherri did. I hadn't talked to her in five years. Wanted to know if I could give her the name of a private investigator." Another bony shrug. "I'd heard you were in the business."

"*You* gave her my name?"

"What did I just say?"

Jack sat back, looked at one wall, then the other, collecting himself. "So you knew this was a scam all along?"

"No, I didn't. I didn't know anything about it, anything but what you told me." He glanced toward the heart monitor. "You get me beating any faster, the nurses'll be in here to kick your ass out."

They were quiet until Norton said, "Don't get a swelled head, bub. I did it for the girl, too. How's she doing, you heard? Tears me up thinking about her in those handcuffs."

Jack leaned forward again and lowered his voice into the breaking-bad-news register. "You need to know this, Norton. She's not your daughter."

"Shit, I know that. I already told you I don't have a daughter. What is it with you? Everything twice."

Jack spread both arms wide. "The records said you were the father of Sherri's baby."

Another wave from Norton. "Go over to the closet there and get my house key out of my pants. I wrote the whole story out for you at home. You can go read it."

"I'm not going to your house to get something you can tell me right now."

"That's where I laid it all out for you, bub, nice and neat."

"Save me a trip." Jack rubbed the back of his neck where Teddy had caught him with the board, and stretched the leg that ached from his tumble over the wall. "I don't want to move around any more than I have to right now."

Norton looked to be thinking it over. "All right." He sighed. "Give me some water."

Jack poured from a plastic pitcher into a paper cup and lifted the clear curtain. Norton took the cup with a shaky hand.

Saying, "The baby girl that Sherri had in nineteen sixty-two?"

He stopped talking and seemed to drift until Jack said, "That's right."

"Near as anyone could tell, I was the father. My wife, Dot, and I adopted her and named her Mary Ann. Beautiful little girl, beautiful. Filled our house up with love, bub."

He took a couple of sips of water. Some of it dribbled from the corner of his mouth, but Norton didn't wipe it away. "Dot could have been bitter about it, you know, but never was, not a day. Knew the whole story about me and Sherri but treated that little girl like her own. . . . Those was some happy years."

Jack waited. Curling white vapor hissed into Norton's tent. Two times Norton opened his mouth, started to talk, then closed it again.

Finally he said, "When she was four years old, we got Mary Ann a bicycle. Tiny little bike, with hard rubber tires and training wheels. Pink and white, had those little plastic tassles hanging from the handlebars. She loved it. Up and down the driveway, every day, up and down, Mary Ann with a big smile on her face."

Norton's voice trailed off. He shook his head under the plastic tent. "Make a long story short, Jack, business associate named Grover Wells come by one day. Him and me had some words 'cause Grover was all pissed about somebody wasn't getting paid that was supposed to."

More hiss of cold air, white vapor. "While Grover Wells and me stood in that driveway shouting at each other about money, I took my eye off Mary Ann."

Norton swallowed, the point of his Adam's apple riding up his throat and back down. Then he lay still, his eyes like lights turned off.

When he started talking again, Jack had to lean close to the tent and watch his lips: "Rode out into the street . . . Neighbor lady on the way to the grocery store . . . Never saw the little girl . . . Four years old . . . Can't imagine how that destroys you."

The room was quiet except for the sound of the air. Jack waited for Norton to pull himself back into the present, the way you wait in the car while someone visits a grave.

After three or four minutes Norton turned his way and said, "So there's your story, bub."

Jack held his stare, afraid if he turned away their talk would be over. "Why didn't you tell me?"

Norton raised a couple of fingers, an almost-shrug. "I

thought about it. I came close a couple times. But I figured Sherri should be the one to let you know. I mean, she's the one that hired you."

Jack didn't talk for a minute. Then: "Norton, if Sandra wasn't yours, why did you go to the edge for her? You risked your life for somebody you didn't even know."

A nod, with eyes closed. "Funny thing. After you came to my house that first time, asking me about my daughter, I started thinking, what if Mary Ann had grown up? What if I'd been watching her like I should have that day?" He raised the cup to his lips and sipped more water, then shook his head a little. "It made me feel good, you know, almost pretending it was really her. And this time I could do it right. This time I wouldn't be looking the other way when she needed me."

Norton reached from under the tent and put a brittle clutch on Jack's hand. "Give you a tip, bub. Sometimes it's not such a bad idea to let yourself be fooled a little bit. Maybe even to fool yourself."

# 29

The sun was setting behind the Strait Lane country estates, with beams slanting through the pampered live oaks, gilding the surfaces of the swimming pools and giving the fake pastures a soft glow. It seemed to Jack they got a better grade of light out here.

At the Omerdome a young man's small army of valet parkers had assembled on the crescent-shaped greystone driveway. They wore white Western shirts and white cowboy hats.

A doorman dressed like the Cisco Kid let Jack into the house. Sherri greeted him with a kiss and "You're the first guest, baby."

They went to the kitchen. Six or seven Mexican women were slicing, pouring, and cooking. Jack looked out the window while Sherri berated the help for not putting enough jalapeños in the bean dip.

In the back yard waiters in white jackets checked place settings at a dozen tables. Two willowy florists in black worried the centerpiece arrangements. A country band tuned up beneath the white lawn tent. And at the edge of the Texas-shaped pool were four young women in bikinis, pulling on the shimmering green fins of their mermaid costumes. The Mermaid of the Pecos had red hair.

As the band, laughing, struck up a hayseed version of "Purple Haze," Sherri was at Jack's elbow. "Let's go have us a talk," she said.

In the Red Room they sat under the paintings of Sherri and the racehorses, just as they had on the day of Jack's first visit. Sherri lit a cigarette as Jack studied her outfit: white low-cut minidress and white leather vest with fringe and a spray of rubies.

"You're handling your grief well," he said.

"Tell you what, people have been calling." She blew smoke at the ceiling. "Calling and saying they're sorry about Dean and is there anything they can do. I'm telling 'em, sure is. Come on to the party, that's what. I've had a boy on the phone all day, dialing the guests. Letting 'em know it doesn't matter one bit what's happened, we're gonna have this party."

Jack waited, making sure she was through. Then he said, "Back to the very beginning, the truth this time. I know she's not yours. Where'd you find her?"

"Find who, baby?"

"Your little girl, as you like to call her."

Sherri smoked, keeping her eyes on Jack. After a while she said, "You figured that much out, good for you."

"Here's what I haven't been able to nail. How did you two get together?"

Sherri blinked twice and took a deep breath. "All right, you deserve it, everything you've been through. Here's the true facts, baby." She closed her eyes for a few seconds, showing him a dreamy smile, and started to talk before she opened them. "About a month ago I took a Caribbean cruise. On the *Sun King*—a beautiful ship, baby, you ever been on it?"

"No."

"Just Sherri, nobody else along, clearing my head for a week, you know? Hey, I'll tell you straight up, I was trying to figure a way outta my marriage. So one night I'm having a cocktail in the ship's lounge, I meet a lovely young woman. Guess who it is. Go ahead, guess."

"Someone enjoying the money she'd ripped off from her elderly parents."

"It was a lovely actress, Miss Sandra Danielle, that's who. On vacation, just like Sherri. Pretty soon, we get to talking . . ." Another smile. "Took us about three rounds to dream the whole thing up. All we had to do was get Sandra to Dallas, call her my long-lost daughter, and let her convince Dean to bite. And baby, he bit hard."

Jack rubbed the side of his face. "All this because you didn't want to stay married? That's why they have divorce courts, Sherri."

"Sure they do, baby. I could've filed on him. Then we would've had us a big messy case, out there for all of Dallas to see. With Dean trying his best to take as much of my money as he could, trying his best to make Sherri look bad. He had nothing to lose, and I had everything. What kind of punishment is that for him?" She winked. "Thank the Lord you did what you did."

She was grinning at him. "Meaning what?" he said.

"That first night? You know what was supposed to happen, don't you?" She gave him a couple of seconds to answer, then rattled her bracelets.

"You're talking about the night he grabbed Sandra outside the coffee bar."

"That's what Sherri just said, baby. See, Dean knew you were there. Sandra told him. So he's thinking him and Sandra'll pretend it's a kidnapping, go on home to his apartment, and wait for Sherri to deliver two hundred thousand in ransom money somewhere."

"After I've told you I've just seen your daughter abducted."

Sherri nodded. "Dumbass Dean thinks Sandra's on his side. But as soon he gets his hands on the ransom money, Sandra plans to call the police and tell 'em she's escaped from her kidnapper. That way, Dean gets arrested, and next morning I go down to the jailhouse and tell him to do the divorce my way—quiet and cheap, I'm talking about—and we won't press charges."

"And I was there that night just to make sure Dean's dirty deed had a witness."

"Some witness." The cigarette bobbed in her mouth. "A witness who goes and jumps in the car and throws everything outta whack."

Jack had nothing to say.

Sherri rattled her bracelets. "Wasn't just Dean, baby, that got all shook up. You knocked us all for a loop. But me and Sandra said, Hey, let's let little old Dean get himself in even deeper. We're thinking: You know what? We got us this detective that wants to ride this horse, let's let him catch Dean doing the whole deal—taking Sandra, locking her up, snapping pictures, asking for ransom, everything. We thought, let's throw this baby into high gear."

"Let Dean dig his hole a little deeper."

"You got it, baby."

"Then it's even easier to hammer him into a settlement. Or else let him get shipped off to prison for a few years."

"On the nose. And thanks to you, it turned out even better. Only thing Sherri has to worry about now is what color casket to get him."

For an instant, Jack flashed on the face of Assistant District Attorney Vanessa Ingram. He remembered again the way she had looked as she clawed at him that last day in her office, with her eyes full of rage and tears. All these years Jack had thought the hatred erupting from her was for him. Now he understood that Vanessa Ingram, at that moment, finally saw what she had become.

"This is for you, baby." Sherri was talking. Jack watched her open the drawer of a lamp table and take out a thick envelope. "Now," she said, "remember I mentioned you had a bonus coming?" She ran her fingers over the white paper of the envelope, a caress. "Twenty-five thousand dollars, how's that sound? For all that good work you did. Will twenty-five thousand get that sour look off your face?"

She sailed it toward him. Flying blood money. The envelope

landed with a fat smack on the rug at his feet. He was staring at it as Sandra walked in. She called to him, voice full of cheer, "Hey, angel-for-hire. You here for the party?"

Sandra wore her own minidress, a black one. On each wrist there were silver bracelets over the blue circles of bruise. Her makeup was heavy enough that it was hard to tell she had been slapped around.

She said, "I'm going back to L.A. tomorrow. Want to go, too?"

Before Jack could respond, Sandra sat next to him and leaned in close. She had on the same perfume she'd worn the night he had dived into the Mustang.

"Come with me," Sandra told him. "Come with me to L.A." Her hand was moving over his thigh as Jack got up to leave.

"Hey," she said, "we can take the train."